JUST ABOUT OVER YOU

CARRIE AARONS

Do you want your **FREE** Carrie Aarons eBook?

All you have to do is **sign up for my newsletter**, and you'll immediately receive your free book!

For every girl who was a real one, and that guy just never saw it. You're beautiful, you're worthy, you're so much better than the person you would have been with him.

PROLOGUE
GANNON

Four Years Ago

Some cheesy slow song starts to lilt the dance floor into coupledom, and I roll my eyes.

My prom date is somewhere off in the bathroom, probably swallowing a teeny tiny pill that will make her go insane at some point. As it is, my own veins buzz with the warmth of three shots of vodka consumed in the school parking lot.

I get that this is some rite of passage for privileged kids in the suburbs, but I've never been that privileged. And this is just another roadblock in my final destination. College, and eventually, Hollywood.

College, where I can finally escape my fucked-up family life. Where I can gain some of the necessary skills and contacts and then pitch myself relentlessly until anything falls into my lap.

This? This is just another night where getting drunk underage is a possibility, and I might be able to get naked with a chick.

Maybe not my prom date, who just stumbled out of the girl's

room. Her eyes rove the floor, and I duck behind one of the pillars in the ballroom. The high school prom committee really outdid themselves, this is a step up from the school cafeteria. Still doesn't mean I want to slow dance with Gia, my date. I brought her mainly to try to get in her pants at the after-party, as bad as that sounds.

But as I spin to avoid detection, my gaze lands on the one girl I actually *did* promise a dance to.

She's standing in the middle of the dance floor, her head swiveling as everyone starts to pair off. The lilac dress she picked swishes around her feet, every single gorgeous ounce of her on display in the sweetest, most innocent way possible.

Oh, how I wanted to be the guy standing behind her while we were all taking pictures at someone's house earlier. How I wished it was me putting that flower corsage on her wrist and helping her up the stairs of the limo bus.

Amelie Brook. The most beautiful girl I've ever seen.

We met when we were ten.

After a horrific breakup that resulted in my half-sister, Desi, being born, my mother moved us from Philadelphia to upstate New York. We landed in Webton, which just so happens to be where Amelie Brook spent her childhood.

I remember the first time I saw her sitting at a desk in the front row of our fifth-grade class; I thought she was Tinker Bell. White-blond hair all swept up in a ponytail, with bangs that swished every time she blinked her eyes. Those eyes were the next thing that captivated me and haven't let me go since.

Brown or maybe amber, some would say, but those are simple terms. Amelie held all of her emotions in them, and I had to physically tear my own gaze from them so many times when we were in the same room.

Nowadays, she still has that mane of moonsilk hair, but it brushes her tailbone and always seems to graze the ass that should have a religion named after it. Jesus fucking Christ, but this girl's curves. They sprang up out of nowhere last year after her boyish figure disappeared. The first day she walked into my house, after seeming to grow D-cups overnight, I had to hide in the bathroom until my dick calmed down. I still find it hard to think away a boner when Amelie is in front of me.

She defines the term hourglass figure, and with how short she is, her perfect tits and drool-worthy ass only seem more exaggerated. Like tonight, when I can't seem to take my eyes off her, no matter how hard I try.

We're best friends, or at least I've put myself in that zone. And as she's my best friend, she is the only girl who could get me to agree to a dance on prom night. Earlier in the week, she made me promise that I'd find her just once, take a sliver of time out of my night for her.

It kills me she thinks I don't want to give her my whole night. Because I do. Fuck, I do. But I know better.

"Come on, let's get out of here!" Sam, the guy in our grade who seems to always be able to score weed, comes up to where I'm standing and hits me in the arm.

I look behind him, and a group of the more popular seniors stand there, including my date. They all look either drunk or high and are itching to leave. The chaperones have to let us out at ten p.m., and a glance at the huge clock on the wall shows me that the time has nearly come.

Glancing back toward the dance floor, I watch as Amelie continues to stand alone. Continues to wait for me. A beat passes, and then another. Then a guy approaches her, some junior whose name I forget. He must ask her to dance because she looks around reluctantly one more time and then shrugs before moving into his embrace.

It's better this way. I should break my promise to her, one of the only ones I've ever made her. I don't make her promises normally, because I know I'll disappoint her. Like this moment. Because I'm not going to dance with her. I'm going to leave and get drunk out of my mind so I can forget the sight of his arms wrapping around her.

If I take her in my arms right now, I'll never let go. And for her benefit, no matter how selfish I am, I'll never do that to her.

I'm the same poison I came from, incapable of a lifelong love.

I've known it since forever; Amelie Brook is way too good for me.

I will never be enough for her. I will never be able to give her the love she deserves. After all, look at the cloth I'm cut from.

Which is why I'll fight every urge to fall for her and resign myself to being the best friend she could ever have.

At least then I can still allow myself to be around her without draining her of the light and goodness she embodies.

1

"I'll see you tomorrow?" Jameson asks, rolling over to pop a quick kiss on my mouth.

I nod, but it's more of a shrug slash non-committal motion. Maybe I'll see him tomorrow. If I feel like it. If my heart and head don't feel so overloaded that they make me chicken out.

"Bye, beautiful." He winks, toeing into his sandals and striding out of my bedroom.

Watching him go as he shuts my door, I flop back onto my pillows. It's the third night, in the two weeks since the fall semester started, that he's slept over. I haven't stayed at his place, and we don't talk more than I'm willing to on any given day.

For now, it's the speed I can handle. Casual hookup with a nice guy who also seems interested in more. After what I've subjected myself to in the love department, I'd say I'm doing pretty well.

It's a typical Friday morning at my version of Talcott University. The private college in Ithaca, New York, is where my two best friends from childhood and I decided to attend school. We spent a year living in the dorms, and then decided to move into a house on Prospect Street, one of the most popular off-campus spots for students. Now that we all turn twenty-one this year, we'll be able to zip right over to the bars across the street and then drunkenly stumble home.

Last night, we threw a small house party for Thirsty Thursday, and I invited Jameson to come over. We've been talking since last semester, around May, and saw each other twice over the summer since he only lives about an hour from my hometown of Webton, which is forty minutes from Talcott. Since getting back to school, not only has Jameson wanted to spend more time together, but I've been open to it.

Which is how he came to wake up in my bed this morning. Things with him are good. Not weird, not awkward. He understood that I have an earlier class this morning and wanted to get a workout in before. He's respectful; the sex is pretty great, and now I can spend my day working and focusing on myself.

I have a paper due next week in my English Literature of the Eighteenth Century course, four books I need to read for a Paranormal Romance class, and I promised my boss at the library that I'd take on an extra shift this weekend. My dream job of working for the New York Public Library is going to be a tough get, but I'm working my butt off to achieve it. Especially since I'm crafting the perfect application for an internship this summer.

While busy dreaming about the smell of all the books in Manhattan, I nearly miss the voices in the hall just outside my door.

"Oh, shit, sorry! Didn't see you there," I hear Jameson say.

Please don't let it be Gannon, please don't let it be Gannon. I squeeze my eyes shut and pray to the gods.

"Uh, no problem. And you are?" That deep rumble has all sorts of skepticism.

Fuck my life. I blow out the breath I was holding.

"Jameson, nice to meet you. I think you were here last night, during the party? I'm, uh, seeing Amelie." He sounds unsure, and I wonder if he'd say that if I was standing next to him.

He doesn't sound like he's bragging or like he wants to hide that we're seeing each other. More like he just doesn't know how to label our relationship, which is probably because of my lax attitude toward it.

"*Are* you?" Gannon says, and I just know the look he has on his face.

A holier-than-thou smirk that could make even the cockiest person cower. The smug bastard, what does he care if I'm seeing someone? It's not like he wasn't promising a girl that he'd marry her mere months ago.

Did I also mention I decided to go to the same college as my guy best friend from back home? Who I also happen to be head over heels in love with? And we all live together in a co-ed, off-campus house?

Because yeah, I am that idiot who agreed to this.

Gannon Raferty. The boy who stole my heart the minute I laid eyes on him in the fifth grade and never gave it back. Unfortunately for me, he has looked at me like a little sister from the jump. That could have been because I basically looked like a kid sister until I miraculously hit puberty junior year of high school.

No, really, I actually don't think I hit puberty until then. I didn't get my period until seventeen. Up until March of junior year of high school, I was flat-chested, had no hips, and genetics had blessed me with the height of a pixie. I'm five one on a good day.

But then something happened, and I grew boobs and a butt overnight. My lips became fuller, the chub in my cheeks dissolved. After that, guys started looking at me differently.

Taya, one-third of our hometown best friend trio and now my college roommate, once told me I look like a mix of Kim

Kardashian and Tinker Bell. It's actually not a far-off comparison.

That's beside the point, though. Gannon has never looked at me with any sort of lust in his eyes, nor has he ever seriously committed to a girl. Until, that is, he was cast on one of the most famous reality TV dating shows in the nation, not to mention the world. He took last semester off to go film it and came in second.

As the runner-up, I had to watch him pick out a ring to possibly propose to a girl he'd known for less than six weeks. Ultimately, she'd turned him down, but a star was born. Now everyone wanted a piece of Gannon, and it's not just me harboring a gigantic, irrational crush on him. It's half the country.

Of course, I watched every episode like the masochist I am. Each week, the knife would turn a little more in my heart. My chest was practically a gaping wound by the end, and Taya and Bevan would have to scrape me up off the couch. They are my best friends; we met in third grade and have been unofficial sisters ever since, and would watch the torture with me no matter how much they disapproved. Taya found the love of her life in Austin last year, and Bevan broke up with her high school sweetheart and our MIA roommate, Callum. And even through all of their relationship problems, they always helped me through my turmoil.

But I'm stronger now. Maybe I had to see that to finally have a come-to-Jesus moment. Gannon is never going to love me or feel anything remotely similar to what I feel for him.

So it's time to move on. I like Jameson, he's the first guy in a while that I feel a small flutter for. And I'm not about to let Gannon moving back into this house screw that up. No matter what my traitorous heart says.

And speaking of getting a move on, I need to. I'm going to

miss the spin class I signed up for at the fitness center if I don't get out of bed now. Quietly, I push off my bed and tiptoe to the door. Like a church mouse, I turn the knob and peek around my door, blowing out a breath when I see that the hall is empty. Gannon and Jameson have left.

I imagine what they must have looked like standing out here. Gannon, the blond muscled demigod with a dimple in his left cheek, a beauty mark just above the right side of his lip, and that Harry Styles-swagger that someone can only be born with and not taught. And then there is Jameson, whose brown hair and brown eyes are nice, if not average. Everything about Jameson is perfectly nice and respectful, the best a girl could ask for. However, we rarely want that, right? It's not what gets our hearts pounding and our panties completely soaked. No, that honor goes to the crooked, come-hither grin that guys like Gannon have mastered.

Fortunately for me, the hallway is empty. Grabbing the workout clothes I laid out yesterday afternoon in preparation for this morning, just in case I was hungover, I race to the shared bathroom and lock myself inside. I could have used the en suite in Taya's bathroom, the only person who has an en suite, but there is the chance she's having FaceTime sex with Austin before he goes in for his midday radio station job, and they need their privacy.

It's fine, I'll deodorant in here, pee, slap some moisturizer on, and change. All of that takes me five minutes, and then I'll grab my school bag, books already packed for today's classes, and run downstairs for a bowl of oatmeal. I'll be out the door in fifteen and be able to put the deep thoughts of this morning behind me.

And if that schedule doesn't tell you all you need to know about me, it should. I'm the kind of person who always has a plan, who never leaves home without looking up the route. I'm planning on being a librarian, order is kind of my life.

I take the stairs two at a time down, something my aunt would yell at me for because I might fall and break my neck. The staircase in our off-campus house is a sweeping menagerie that is typically littered with drunken students on Friday and Saturday nights.

The house is made up of four floors. The basement is the drinking games zone. Then there is the first floor with its massive living room decked out with cathedral ceilings, the kitchen with its massive butcher block island in the center, a dining room that is the constant location of every roommate studying together, and a powder room that we rotate cleaning. The second floor houses every bedroom, five in total, besides the attic. The attic is Gannon's space, a bachelor pad open-concept room that spans the entire length of the house. Last semester, Austin, Taya's boyfriend, sublet it while Gannon was filming the show.

Typical for Talcott, our college that stands on the hill atop a massive Finger Lake, the house has an antique vibe to it, with scuffed chestnut hardwood and crown molding everywhere. It looks more like a Victorian-era dollhouse than a place where kids get shitfaced every weekend, but that's the charm.

As I turn the corner into the kitchen, I see Bevan standing at the stove, her back to me.

"Morning," I singsong in my typical chipper tone.

Bev grunts at me, which is her usual a.m. greeting. She is not a morning person by any stretch, and with the way her life has been, I kind of don't blame her for the constant gloom. Callum, her high school sweetheart and our housemate, moved out at the end of last semester after their breakup. They've been on and off for years, but this one seems like it's sticking, and she's been a wreck. Of course, she'll never say that, but I hear her crying at night on the other side of the wall we share.

What I don't realize is that Gannon is perched on the counter, an apple in his mouth as he texts someone. And he's shirtless. I have to physically make myself not look in his direction, or I won't stop staring.

"You want a ride to campus?" I ask Bevan, hooking my arms around her waist in a hug as she stirs her eggs.

"Yeah, thanks." She leans back into me.

We've been each other's source of comfort for years. Taya is our third, the glue, but Bevan and I relate more to each other. After all, we both come from broken homes. While Taya has her drama with her parents and sister, their family unit is intact and solid.

"Morning." Gannon hops down, apparently done with being sucked into his phone.

I can't stand that mobile device that seems attached to his hand. Even before he went to film the show, he was addicted to it. Always texting random girls, checking his social media incessantly, always needing another hit of attention from whatever was on that screen.

Personally, I rarely even bother looking at my phone. All the love I need is right here in front of me, aside from my aunt back in Webton. Who do I need to impress?

No, paperbacks are my form of entertainment. If I'm in a pinch, I'll grab my Kindle, but I usually always have a stray book in my bag if I need a distraction.

Ignoring Gannon, I go to the cabinet where I keep my food and pull out a nut and fruit granola bar. The six of us all have one cabinet in the kitchen designated as our own, so there isn't too much food sharing or stealing.

"Great, glad to know we're still not talking." He makes a sarcastic pfft sound.

I haven't really spoken to him in any real length since before he left for the reality show. I was so heartbroken about it and that he'd be leaving for four months that I could barely acknowledge him. By the time he returned to campus during the week of final exams last spring, I wasn't just heartbroken. I was furious. Gannon showed up at the house unexpectedly and strolled in like a soldier returning from war. He expected some warm reunion, but instead, I'd punched him in the stomach and ran away to hide in my room.

Nothing has been the same since. I spent all summer completely avoiding him in our hometown and even hid behind a display of pillows at Target when he happened to be in the store at the same time as me.

"I'd love if anyone could fill me in on why you all hate me." That deep voice vibrates through me.

"Oh, come on, you know that." Taya strolls in, her graceful, chill mood defusing some of the tension.

"Good morning," I tell her, giving Gannon a pointed look as if to demonstrate that I'm never going to wish him the same.

And he does know why we hate him. Or at least he has to know a little bit. If he doesn't, he's dumber than even we gave him credit for.

"I heard Jameson leave this morning." Taya smiles at me. "He's such a sweetheart."

My lips turn up into a smile because he really is. But before I can answer, we're interrupted.

"That guy is a chump, Ams."

The nickname he's used for me since elementary school has always melted a part of me. Now it just grates, picking away at the barely formed scabs he left on my heart. And the fact that he's picking on Jameson really pisses me off.

"Funny, a lot of people would say that about you." I glower, crossing my arms over my chest.

Gannon's jaw drops. I know why, too. I've never been this direct, this blunt, when it comes to him.

"Well, well … maybe you shouldn't have him sleeping over. I think he's beneath you."

Bevan and Taya turn, ready to come to my defense, or maybe Jameson's, but I put a hand up. This one I have a comeback for, and it's rolling off my tongue before I can even stop to check my rage.

"And maybe you shouldn't be telling women you've known for six weeks that you're going to marry them. Then again, with your thirst for fame, I guess it's not beneath you."

The shock I see cross his face couldn't be more apparent than if I slapped him. Which I've thought about, but my punch last spring made me so ashamed that I'll never physically touch him like that again. But he's so stunned he can't even respond, and I think his puny brain might be malfunctioning.

Before we can get into it further, I pick up my school bag and granola bar and then turn to blow kisses to my best friends.

It should feel better telling him off. I should be puffing my chest out with pride as I walk to my car, slam the driver's side door, and crumple with my forehead to the steering wheel.

But it doesn't. I'm not. Because being mean isn't in my nature, especially when it comes to Gannon.

No, the only thing I feel are the thousands of cuts those episodes of his dating show left on my heart. They haven't healed one bit, no matter how much I throw myself into another relationship.

The boy I fell for in fifth grade still has the ability to destroy me, and until I can figure out how to get him out of my system, any way I try to move on is already doomed from the start.

2

My middle finger is flying high as the guy retreats down the stairs, still buttoning his shirt into place. Fucking prick.

Since when does Amelie have guys coming out of her room in the morning? Since when does Amelie let guys sleep over?

Apparently, I missed a lot since I was gone all last semester.

With the taste of toothpaste still in my mouth, I pad down the stairs, checking to see if Jameson vacated the premises. On the way down, I pull out my phone and check my socials. A thousand new followers on Instagram, two thousand on TikTok, and two emails about partnering with influencer brands.

I didn't get engaged on the reality TV dating show I was cast for last spring, and now I'm making money posting teeth whitening ads on my social media. I'd say life is pretty fucking good.

The house is quiet, it's still early on this Friday morning, but I can't sleep. I barely drank last night, was up with a million thoughts in my head, and since getting back from filming the show, the shooting schedule and jet lag have really messed up my schedule.

There are remnants in the hall from the small house party my roommates held that lasted into the morning hours, and I step over red Solo cups, puddles of liquor, and even a girl's top. Hopefully, that top belongs to one of the girls who lives here, but it's possible that Scott, my only other male roommate at this time, had someone sleep over. Scott is notorious for sleeping around.

For a house that throws a crap ton of parties, we actually have a relatively clean and comfortable space most of the time. But the rest of the house got up to some mischief last night, and it shows. Me? I could barely down a shot. Things haven't felt right since I got back to Talcott. Both in my friend's group and internally. I feel like a fish out of water and can't seem to slide back into the groove. I've always been able to do that; I'm a chameleon. I fit in anywhere, can charm anyone, and usually feel completely comfortable in my own skin.

But not recently.

I have a feeling that my best friend, if she even qualifies as that anymore, probably has something to do with that. Or maybe it's the complete tool I bumped into coming out of her room this morning.

When I make it down there, the kitchen is empty of anyone except for Bevan. Yippee. One of Amelie's two best friends, though I would prefer Taya because at least she won't try to rip my testicles from my body. Bevan is not only one of the feistiest females I've ever met, but she actually scares me, and that's on a good day, and she's been going through a horrific breakup with Callum, one of my best friends. So yeah, I don't want to touch her with a ten-foot pole.

But I do want information on the asshole I just ran into on my way back from the bathroom.

Amelie has been the closest person to me since we were ten. Since the day I met her in fifth grade when I showed up in my tattered jeans and jacket that was two sizes too small. No one else seemed to want to have anything to do with me, but then there was this little angel. A pip-squeak of a thing, with beautiful blond hair as white as the driven snow and eyes the color of chocolate melting into caramel. She was so sweet and asked me if I wanted one of her feather pens she was writing with. Somewhere, I still have that blue puff of a writing utensil.

We've grown up together, been there for every hard and wonderful moment. I was the one who cradled her in my arms at her parents funeral in sixth grade. She was the one who fed me pudding after I had my appendix out sophomore year of high school. We took trips to the lake and spent nights sitting in the local frozen yogurt shop.

She has been my person. Even more than the girls are to her, I am her constant. Coming from the background I do, promoted to the man of the family before I even knew what that was, Amelie was this pure, sweet creature that I got to lean on and keep all to myself.

But then I went to do the show, and it changed everything. Apparently, irrevocably.

"Who's the guy Amelie is ... *seeing*?" I use his word, the guy I found in the hallway, for whatever they were doing in her bedroom last night.

A big green monster sits on my back, and it feels like he's squeezing my heart between his hands. Almost as if he could make it pop from the ache coursing through it. Thinking about that guy in her bed makes me want to tear the whole house down.

"You're a fucking douche." Bevan grunts and turns back to the stove.

"Good morning to you too, Bev." I chuckle, but her greeting leaves another cut on my soul.

Those are the only four words she's uttered since I got back from the reality dating show I was selected to go on.

Mrs. Right is a spinoff of the hugely popular dating show, *Mr. Right*. There is one main woman, on my season it was Cassandra, who has twenty-five men selected for her to date. At the end, she picks one to presumably get engaged to.

I was the youngest guy ever cast on a season at the age of twenty-one. There was a lot of speculation about that on social media and among viewers about if I was serious, but I played my role to the tee. A bit inexperienced when it comes to love, the sob story about no dad in my life, and an overall charm that none of the other guys exuded.

I knew I had the game on lock from day one. The moves and routes seemed easy to get to the end, and producers wanted to tee me up to possibly appear on the show again. I had a good time with it—and Cassandra. She was an accomplished woman, a twenty-six-year-old lawyer who owned a home in Charlotte, North Carolina, and ran marathons for fun. Cass wasn't someone I'd necessarily rule out dating, but I had no intention of actually marrying her, despite what I said.

Do I feel bad for leading her on? For fooling America into thinking I wanted to pop the question and get down on one knee? No. It was all makeup and Hollywood. The entire show wasn't real. Hell, the guy she picked already publicly cheated on her and they've since broken up. I'm not even sure Cass was ready to settle down since she used the show to promote the skincare line she just came out with.

No one got hurt, and everyone pretty much got what they wanted. At least, I thought I had. Since the age of three, I've had people telling me I was destined for stardom. That I had *it*, whatever *it* is. When the *Mrs. Right* producers cast me on the spot at an open call audition, I thought it was destiny.

And I've gotten what I wanted. Brand deals that are making me more money than a job in marketing using my degree ever could. Influencer status that lands me free products, clothes, and food so that I never have to be the scrawny poor kid ever again.

Somehow, though, I feel emptier than before.

Amelie wanders into the kitchen, and I have to contain my groan of frustration. It's bad enough I've had to rebuff her feelings and hide mine for years on end. But to have to pretend like I'm not attracted to the most killer body I've ever seen with my two eyes? It's torture.

She's wrapped in these pink workout leggings that highlight the ass I'd commit crimes for to get my hands on. Her height is pixie-ish, which only serves to turn me on more because it would be so easy to toss her around during sex. That tiny little waist has always taunted me, and her flat stomach just begs my tongue to lick across it.

But it's her boobs that have always rendered me speechless. They shouldn't be legal for a girl of her height. More than a handful each, I've fantasized about putting my face between them and breathing in the sweet scent of her sweat while I pound into her.

Fuck, I need to get myself under control. It's only eight in the morning, and I'm now sporting a raging hard-on in the middle of the kitchen.

So I pretend to duck my head in my phone as I recite the Pledge of Allegiance in a whisper. I don't miss the way she looks me up and down with the eyes that I have memorized for years. Every fleck of gold in the caramel, the way they register things, and the way they look when she's daydreaming.

Right now, Amelie is boring those eyes into my phone. I know how she hates that I spend so much time on the thing.

"Morning," I say, being a little too smug, jumping down off the counter.

If I'd just come off it, actually apologize for the reason I know she's mad at me, then we could squash this. But if I admit that I know, I open up an entire can of worms.

Because to this day, Amelie believes I'm oblivious to the feelings she has for me. Apologizing for telling another girl that I want to marry her on national television will make it more than a bit obvious that I've known all along.

Taya walks into the kitchen at this moment, and says, "I heard Jameson leave this morning. He's such a sweetheart."

Before Amelie can even respond, the words are out of my mouth. "That guy is a chump, Ams."

I can't help it. She's ignoring me, and I want to get a rise out of her. I've told her for years how she deserves the best of the best. I don't even know the guy, but I know by looking at him that he's not good enough for her.

"Funny, a lot of people would say that about you." Amelie glowers, crossing her arms over her chest in a way that has my eyes zeroing right in on her cleavage.

But her words feel like a knife to the gut. I know why, too. She never talks to me like this. It's a shock to the system.

"Well, well ... maybe you shouldn't have him sleeping over. I think he's beneath you." The comeback is weak, and I'm grasping.

Amelie is all barely-contained rage as she sets about whipping with her tongue.

"And maybe you shouldn't be telling women you've known for six weeks that you're going to marry them. Then again, with your thirst for fame, I guess it's not beneath you."

Fucking *ouch*. That verbal spar feels like she reached into my chest and ripped my goddamn heart out.

I know why they're pissed. Why my best friend won't talk to me and why she punched me the first time she saw me when I came back to school.

Instead of being at Talcott, instead of telling her how I really feel about her, I chose a show and a girl I barely knew. I confessed feelings, ones I never had, to a woman I only just met because some TV producer told me to. Because if I did so, I'd gain more clout, more fame. I might be able to make a name for myself and get far away from the shitty situation I'd grown up in by leveraging that fame for money.

Let's get one thing straight, I'm not an oblivious moron. I'm well aware of why Amelie can barely look at me. As if seeing the heartbreak right there in her eyes doesn't gut me daily.

But I've never once led her on, lied to her, or intentionally done anything to hurt her.

I guess I thought I could just come back and we'd patch up the awkwardness. Now I see I was naive as fuck for thinking that.

Especially since it appears that she's finally tried to start something with another guy. I know how wrong it is that I'm furious, jealous, and lashing out at her. But seeing Jameson come out of her room ignited something in me.

Amelie rushes from the kitchen, and I hear the front door slam. Releasing a breath, it feels like my lungs are full of glass. Bevan and Taya stand there, trying to put me six feet under with their glares.

My Apple Watch dings on my wrist. It was a present for myself after the show ended. To celebrate getting some fame, some money, and not being engaged to a girl I barely knew, only to further my career. Some would call me a cold-hearted bastard that I'd resort to that, but they didn't know my story. So fuck them for judging.

The alarm, though, tells me I have about twenty minutes to make it to my first class. And while I'm usually lax about that shit, I can't be this semester. I'm taking more credits this semester and next to make up for missing the last spring academic year.

Being a marketing major is a breeze for me, but I'm going to have to buckle down. Despite what people might think because of how I look, I have a 3.8 GPA, and school has always come pretty easy. I'm not honors level like Taya, or kick-ass at everything I try, like Bevan. But I am smarter than people give me credit for.

I'll have to use that to my advantage, because I have a lot of ground to make up.

In all areas of my life, it seems.

Pushing the strawberry, coated in balsamic around the bowl, I get lost in my head while poking at my salad.

"You going to eat that, or should we talk about it?" Taya asks gently.

The bustle of the Sunrise Diner moves all around us, but our corner booth in the back is like a little cloud of gloom.

"What is there to talk about?" I sulk, stabbing a piece of lettuce.

"Yeah, if she wants to cower in her self-deprecation, let her." Bevan gives Taya a mean glare.

"Or we could discuss how she handed Gannon his balls this morning." Taya shrugs, picking up her burger and biting a hunk of cheesy goodness off.

If I ate like she did, I'd be a balloon. I'm not one who is overly conscious about my weight, and generally like eating plant-based, but I envy Taya sometimes. She eats like a trucker on a road trip, all grease and carbs, and still looks like a stick. If I eat an extra cookie after dinner, I'm bloated for the rest of the week.

The lunch rush at Sunrise, our favorite off-campus eatery

that overlooks the enormous lake that almost swallows our college town, isn't something we're usually present for. Breakfast is more our jam, but we haven't gone grocery shopping this week, and I didn't feel like heading home to fix myself something. So I texted my two best friends, and here we are, sulking over salads.

"He's so infuriating." I grind my teeth together in anger.

"That he is. Always so smug, that one. I want to take his phone and throw it against the wall." Bevan gets an evil glare in her eye.

"I feel like, if you'd just talk to him—" Taya tries to make me see reason.

"Tay, he hurt me. I won't say worse than anyone ever has, because well ..."

They know the worst moment of my life. They were the ones picking me up off the floor each day in the weeks after my parents died. I'll never forget the sound of the sirens wailing through Webton. They woke me from my sleep, and I ran downstairs to my aunt Cheryl, who had been babysitting me. When my mom's sister got the call, I remember collapsing into a ball and barely being able to get out of that position for days.

"We know." Bevan breaks her angry mold and wraps an arm around my shoulder.

The table is silent for a few beats, and then I say, "Let's talk about something else."

"I miss Austin." Taya sighs, and we both whip our heads to look at her. "What?"

"No. Not right now. You don't get to go all lovey-dovey cry fest over here. I'm reeling from a breakup and she's having passive-aggressive word battles with her non-boyfriend, ex-best friend. We don't want to hear about how much of a struggle it is for you to have phenomenal FaceTime sex. We don't want to hear about how your perfect boyfriend writes you love letters and how tough it was leaving him after living a dream life in New York City for the summer."

"Okay, Bev, a bit harsh?" I warn her off.

I might be upset, but Bevan is in a category all her own. She's critical and blunt by nature, but lately, it has been over the top. I guess that's what happens when the love of your life moves out and breaks off your relationship. But Taya has worked hard for her relationship. They had a lot of struggles at the beginning, and I know how much she misses him now that they're doing the long-distance thing.

Taya takes Bevan's hand. "I'm sorry, you're right."

Taya is the best of us. She's not a doormat like me, nor is she always wearing brass knuckles like Bev. She flows easily, moving from one emotion to another without getting stuck in a grudge or letting things fester for years on end. Like I've done with Gannon.

"No, I'm being a bitch. Sorry," Bevan grumbles and lets her head sink into her hands.

"Let's do something fun this weekend. Just the three of us," I suggest.

"Throwing darts at a picture of Callum's face?" She perks up.

"Admitting to Gannon why we're mad at him so I can stop avoiding him in the house?" Taya looks hopeful.

I have to chuckle because apparently, we're on the sarcastic parade this morning.

"I was thinking more like mani-pedis, but those work, too. Actually no, the Gannon one is a no-go." I frown.

"Mani-pedis sounds good. I need one of those pedicures where they put that orange wax on your heels. My feet look like dinosaur hooves." Taya makes a disgusted face.

"You could use my foot file. It's in the shower in the shared bathroom." Bevan pops a piece of grilled chicken in her mouth.

"The only thing grosser than thinking about grating my foot

skin like cheese, is using a file that's already been used by someone else to do so."

I nod in agreement. "Yeah, that sounds nasty as hell."

The three of us break into giggles, and I'm reminded why I love these two. Not that I'm not reminded constantly anyway. When we decided to come to college together, so many people judged us. I even had a couple of people tell me I was lucky to bring built-in friends to college since I don't branch out much. That stung.

The truth is, we just love each other. They're my sisters. We're all still growing and learning, coming into our own, but I love that I get to do so by their sides. I wouldn't be surprised if we all end up in New York City after graduation. Taya is most definitely headed there to work as a translator for the United Nations, since she interned there this summer and knocked it out of the park. And if I get this internship with the library, I'm hoping it means an actual job after I get my diploma.

As for Bevan? Who knows. She could go on to be some coach for a professional athletic team or a lawyer. She's double majoring in legal studies and sports media, but the girl could conquer the world with just her pinky if she set her mind to it. Her problem is narrowing down what she actually wants out of life.

Through it all, though, we're each other's family.

"Not grosser than the time you borrowed the shorts I wore after Callum and I had sex for the first time." Bevan points a finger at Taya.

"Okay, first of all, I had no idea you'd worn those to lose your virginity. Second of all, you could have told me!"

Our waitress comes by to check on us, and we all order another round of chocolate milk. No matter how old we are, or what meal it is, chocolate milk is our unifier. It's the thing that will always make us feel better, and today seems like a two-round kind of day.

"Are we having a party tonight?" I muse.

"Definitely. I need to get blackout." Bevan nods.

That sounds like a horrible idea for her right now, but I'll still let her do it and be the one holding her hair when she pukes.

"Scott already texted me saying he invited a few friends."

"In Scotty language, that means fifty." I chuckle.

Scott, our sixth roommate, is a ladies' man and the life of the party. He's the only roommate who didn't go to Webton but fits into our little family as if he's always been here. And now, I guess he's our fifth roommate, since Callum is nowhere to be found.

Our house is one of the hottest properties at Talcott. We scooped up Six Prospect Street in a hurry when it became available our sophomore year. Not only is it huge, and perfect to throw parties, but it's right near The Commons, or the village of shops and bars down the hill from the university. Which means that this year, when we all turn twenty-one, besides Gannon, who already is, we can easily stumble home from the bars at 2:00 a.m.

"I'm fine with it." I shrug, because I'm usually down for a party.

It's college, and we're only here once, so we might as well make the most of our weekends.

"Are you going to invite Jameson over again?" Taya wiggles her eyebrows.

Honestly, I haven't thought about him since he left this morning. Which is probably a bad sign, right? Almost immediately, my mind had gone to Gannon when I heard him and Jameson out in the hallway. Then it never left my infuriating former best friend while he accosted me in the kitchen and supplanted these angry thoughts.

"I'm not sure. Two nights in a row is a lot."

"Says the only one of us getting laid. You really should take advantage." Bevan smiles.

A blush heats my cheeks. "I don't mean sex, gosh, you're so dirty. I mean, we just spent all night together last night. We're not together or anything. It could come off as clingy, or too strong."

"Um, have you seen the way the guy looks at you? He'd love for you to cling to him." Taya pffts.

She must see the way my face goes white, because I didn't realize they saw Jameson looking at me any type of way. I can see Taya backpedaling, but the damage is done. They know how slow I want to take this, and my best friends see all. They don't miss a thing when it comes to me.

Which means Jameson is more invested than I initially thought. And that scares me.

"You're casual. You don't need to rush anything. It's new and fun and he's a great guy. You've been plagued by this thing for Gannon for ages, and adjusting to liking a new person is going to feel weird. I think what you're doing is perfectly fine. Plus, who wants a man to worry about all the time?"

Taya sticks her tongue out as if she's mocking herself. And probably to make me feel better about not having to be so serious with Jameson. I don't tell her this, but it only makes me feel worse. I want a man to worry about. And that man I want, he's a specific one whose name does not start with a J. I want the man I've loved for as long as I can remember to worry about me, not to mention love me back.

My feelings for Gannon are always top of mind and top of heart. As if they're intermingled with my breaths, or they're one with the beat of the organ keeping me alive.

Splicing those out might kill me. But it's looking more and

4

GANNON

The water of Second Dam flows in a green-brown trickle over the waterfall, the murky waters winking at me from up on the cliff.

Below, dozens of Talcott students tan themselves on the rocks, the sun shining through the forest of trees shielding this gorge from the outside world. It's a peaceful part of nature that we've infested with ego, beer cans, and girls in string bikinis. But hey, I'm not complaining.

It's a hike to get up here, almost a mile into the woods and up the mountains that make up the back of campus. Students do it in their sneakers and bathing suits, carrying towels around their necks, for the scene and the thrill of the jump. The gorges are a Talcott staple, it's practically the first thing every freshman does on their first weekend here. Hike to the cliffs and lake and then jump off into the water. There is a twenty-foot jump, a forty-foot jump, and a sixty-foot jump.

Right now, a girl is standing on the ledge of the twenty, squealing and batting her eyelashes at the guy behind her. She's partly scared but also wants him to comfort her. Ninety percent sure he'll go back to her dorm room tonight.

The twenty is the most common, the easiest of jumps. It's for those who want to say they jumped rather than pussied out and sat on the rocks. The forty is for those more daring, who want a little thrill but still aren't willing to completely risk their lives just to look cool.

And then there is the sixty. The jump barely anyone attempts because you could break a body part or jump too far to the left and actually tumble down the waterfall rocks. It's stupid and irrational to jump, a complete risk that could land you in the hospital. But if you pull it off, you're golden here on campus. A legend. People *know* you.

Which is exactly why I come here to jump from that height.

I jumped from the sixty on my first trip here as a freshman. Climbed right up those rocks and flung my body off without thinking. Now that I've done it, felt the thrill, had the water engulf me as I plummeted, there is no going back.

I'm here alone today, because Callum is a recluse these days, and Scott is off with his latest fuck buddy. I have no problem doing things alone. Honestly, I'm better that way. I have friends, and I'm always in a group because of how I look, though that sounds shallow. But I don't let people close to me. Amelie was really the first, and almost only, one who was allowed past my walls.

And with good reason. It's hard to let people fully connect to you when you'll just end up moving somewhere else shortly after.

My mom had me when she was sixteen. Growing up in rural Virginia, sex and drugs were the only things to get up to, apparently, and she'd fallen into both. By the time she had me, my father, a twenty-seven-year-old who wasn't waiting around for a baby or the statutory rape charges, had split.

From there, we lived with my grandmother for three years. I know this because Mom told me, not because I remember it.

Then it was on to Philadelphia, where my sister, Quinn, was born the day before Mom turned twenty.

With two kids and just shy of the drinking age, Mom was struggling. We lived on food stamps, unemployment, and money she could make doing God knows what. I don't ask about those times because they were dark as fuck, and I knew that, even though I was four at the time.

Another move brought us to Tampa, where she met Freddie, her first husband. He was a used car salesman with a bad toupee, but he wasn't bad to us. Neglectful, with a raging adultery problem, but he put us up, and we finally had beds to sleep in. They got pregnant with Mallory when Mom was twenty-two, and then a year later had my brother, Alwin.

Four kids are a lot for any family, but Freddie couldn't hang with so many mouths to feed. Especially when two weren't his. And it wasn't as if he and Mom weren't cheating on each other. She'd go out three nights a week to meet other men, even daring to bring one or two home while we were there and Freddie wasn't.

Eventually, he took off, leaving us with his bills and Mom with zero money.

During the years with Freddie, though, Mom had time to study and pass her GED. Add in some administration courses at a local community college, and she was actually able to land her first steady job when we got to Philadelphia after fleeing Tampa. She was working as a receptionist at a Fortune 500 company when she met Lyle.

Lyle was a decent guy. Rich as fuck, and probably didn't want kids in his life, but he genuinely cared for my mom and didn't treat us kids badly. She got pregnant with Fiona just a month after their quickie wedding at the Philly court house. So there we were, a collection of half-siblings all trudging along through life while our mom lived out her teens and twenties she never got. She and Lyle went on boat trips, leaving us with a nanny we'd never met. They'd go out and come back during the wee hours of the morning.

Sure, we were living in an upscale house on the Main Line, but we were all still as neglected and uncomfortable as usual. I was older by then and knew Mom's game. She loved, in her own way, but she was still cheating on her husband. And so came Fitz, my youngest sibling, who I'm pretty sure is not Lyle's son at all.

Mom almost died during the surgery trying to have him, and the doctors could barely save her. That was the second period of dark days. She had to have a hysterectomy and didn't get herself out of bed for months. We weren't being taken care of, and I ended up having to step up. I'd get my brothers and sisters on the bus, rock Fitz when he cried, or make him a bottle in the middle of the night. I was the one who brought Mallory to her speech therapist when she developed a stutter from the lack of parenting going on in our home.

When Lyle died four years into their marriage, Mom was beside herself. She didn't truly love him, but our life had been okay, I guess. It was probably the best her life had been, well, *ever*.

Then began the battle with his family over his estate, which Mom eventually won. He left her everything, including his three-million-dollar savings account. That's how we've survived for a while, then after Mom blew through most of the money, she worked reception jobs. She moved us to Webton after the court cases were done, and the rest is history.

And that's my whole sad family saga. Six kids, a mother who didn't know how to properly love, and not a dad in sight.

My mom is a good mom ... I guess. She loves us, in her way, and has always tried to never let us go hungry or without a roof over our heads. But it's no wonder that I'll never be able to settle down. That I can't give a real, honest woman a chance.

And when I think of who that woman would be, Amelie's face pops into my mind.

Not only is adultery in my blood, but so is leaving. Amelie is the type of girl who, before her parents passed, came from the ultimate American family. White picket fence, doting mother and father, dinner every night as a family with salad dressings on the table. They read her stories and tucked her in. I know that if they were alive, they'd be the parents recording the entire graduation ceremony on an iPad and sobbing when they dropped her off for college.

As opposed to my mother, who gave me a pack of cigarettes for my car to drive to Talcott with. I have no idea what true love or everlasting companionship looks like. I've been terrified for ten years that I'll simply mess up our friendship. I'm that nervous about what runs through my veins.

Who could blame me? I have both daddy *and* mommy issues. I'm so fucked in the head, I can barely keep a casual acquaintance.

A bunch of students are buzzing around the forty-foot jump. The guys are trying to hype each other to jump off, and the girls are standing around trying to flaunt their bodies before flinging themselves from the rocks.

I see where they are jumping from and bypass it, choosing instead to use my hands and feet to pull myself up to the sixty-foot ledge. There are not many places to stand up here, which is fine because there is only one other kid attempting this today. He looks back, spots me, and then focuses before jumping off to do a gainer backflip. I don't see him hit the water, but I hear it, and below, the cheers are obviously for him.

Kid has style. I'm not sure if I'll flip today or if I'll just dive headfirst. I never just jump. Too obvious. Too easy. If this is the thing that can wake me up from my weirdness at the moment, then I'm going to give it all I've got.

I don't look down as my bare feet inch out onto the rocks, the clay and stone rough beneath my soles. Before I can think, I'm launching myself in an arc, my arms straight out in front of me before they swoop over my head.

The water slaps my entire body like I'm being hit with a thousand rubber bands at once. I flinch, my body twitching as the icy water engulfs me. It might be early September, one of the warmest times in upstate New York, but the water is frigid. The dark green color takes on an inky black hue as I sink further and further, my face and chest aching from the way I hit the water.

The pain is good; it brings something. A feeling, any kind of feeling, is good right now. There is a lot I've been lying to myself about, but being back at Talcott in my usual spots ... it brings some sense of normalcy.

When I surface, the cheers have already erupted. People have their phones out, no doubt posting this to social media. They're waving and pointing, and I hear a bunch of them mention my name. I'm known here as *the dating show guy*, and I can't say I hate it. The past couple of weeks since the semester started, I've had no less than fifty people approach me for autographs.

That, along with the praise now, has me preening like a peacock. This is the feeling I've been searching for. Being recognized, being known, being desired ... it's a hell of a lot better than not being those things.

I grew up most of my life being told I was unwanted or just completely neglected.

Finally, I'm being noticed.

But it's the little voice in the back of my head questioning if it's by the right people and what that means in the long run.

5

AMELIE

"Someone is swinging from the chandelier above the stairs."

A wisp of a conversation catches my ear as I make my way to the basement, and I roll my eyes. I love the parties we have at our house, but sometimes they get too out of hand. Like tonight. It's not even 10:00 p.m. and already there is a vibe that shit is going to get chaotic and weird.

People are too drunk, and the entire house smells like someone is attempting to hotbox it. I saw a girl getting finger-banged on the dance floor, and I'm sure there is more weird sexual shit going on in the corners of the basement. I'm just glad I locked the door to my room and the key is in my back pocket. I don't need anyone having orgasms on my sheets except for me, of course.

I'm not about to knock people for getting a little ape shit, but this feels like it's quickly turning into a "call the cops" night, and I don't want to deal with that.

But instead of doing something, I keep moving toward the basement. The lights are off, and I can only make out my way down from touching the walls and the flashes of light from the strobes Scott installed. Why that was a necessity, I'll never know, but at least it keeps me from breaking my neck.

By the time I make it to the bar, intent on forgetting this night just as much as the next person, dismay fills me. Gannon is holding court behind the wooden structure that has existed in the basement long before we lived here. Girls are cozied up next to it, flirting shamelessly, while his fan club of bros cheers him on while he juggles a liquor bottle.

I hope he drops it and cuts his hand on the glass.

God, too harsh. But I'm so frustrated with him and this whole situation. I wish we could just erase last semester and go back to when I pretended I wasn't deeply in love with him, and he had no clue that I'd give up the world to be with him.

Not that he knows that now. But he does know I'm pissed. And eventually, it's going to come out that I'm mad because of the things he said to that other woman.

Bypassing his cheering section, I find an empty, half-decent chair a little further into the basement. I don't know what has me in a mood tonight. I should go find Bevan and Taya and take a shot or something, but I can't seem to stop sulking.

A couple minutes later, a hand is visible in the strobe lights, holding out a drink to me.

"Made you a pineapple vodka." Gannon hands me the cup as people begin to filter upstairs into the living room.

"Thanks," I grumble, drinking it.

God, I hate him. Even the drink tastes sweeter because he made it.

"You know what they say about eating pineapple." Gannon wiggles those bushy blond eyebrows.

I get lost in his gaze, the flirty smirk directed solely at me is way too powerful for its own good.

"No?" I say, because I really don't.

"It makes you taste sweeter. Down there." His eyes travel low, past my navel, and land between my thighs.

It's as if I'm completely naked, and I feel my entire body blush.

I'm an amateur when it comes to sex. I've only had two partners. A guy our freshman year who barely lasted long enough the couple of times we did it for me to feel anything. And Jameson. Who is better, much better, but we've only ever done missionary. Wait, we did doggy-style once and I felt so weird that we switched back.

The things that Gannon probably knows about sex could be put into an anthology. A very thick one. I used to hear rumors about him in high school, and I'd burn with jealousy and naivety.

Now, here he is, talking about how a fruit can make me taste sweeter if a guy's mouth were between my legs. I could faint on the spot.

"I'll have to ask Jameson if that's true." I give him a snide smile, feeling my cockiness puff my chest out.

Gannon's gaze flicks to my cleavage, fully visible in my white tank top with lacy flowers swirling all over. Huh. That's new. I don't think I've ever seen him check me out. Nonetheless, I steel my heart against the flutters that go through me at the possibility.

After taking his time blazing a blush into my chest, he flicks his eyes back up. They're barely visible in the basement, even though he's now crouching down next to the chair I'm occupying. That doesn't matter, though. I've had them memorized since I was ten.

Chocolate, the kind smooth enough to melt on your fingers if you hold it a half-second too long. Intense in their gaze, like they're always a step ahead. Hiding so many things he doesn't want the world to see.

I used to know all those secrets. But these days, it feels like we couldn't be further apart.

"Where *is* what's his name tonight?" Gannon's voice is a growl.

I chuckle. "Stop it. You know his name. He told you it himself, and I *just* said it. Don't do that."

Charming Gannon comes out now, smirking at me in that irresistible way. "Do what?"

"Pretend you don't know his name just because I'm seeing someone." I scowl. "And don't do that either. The whole 'melt your attitude' smile. I know it too well. You're ..."

I'm about to say my best friend but stop myself. Those words seem cheap in light of the recent developments in our relationship. And when I used to say them, before the show, they'd gut me each time. I didn't want to be his friend.

"We should talk, Ams." He reaches out and touches my hand.

The contact is a shock, it's been so long since I've felt his skin on mine. Back before the show, he used to hug me all the time. He'd wrap his arm around my shoulder, walking me to class or graze my hand with his in goodbye. I would live for those moments.

But since he got back, I've kept him at arm's length. Because I know that if he touches me, I'll be a goner.

Like I am now, leaning into him even though it's just his palm on the top of my hand. Reading way too much into this minimal touch.

Gannon shifts, and I feel him lean in too. Our mouths are inches apart, and the ringing in my ears drowns out the noise of the basement. This is the first time since I've known him that I can feel him looking at me with something other than friendly amusement.

The expression on his face ... I've seen it before. When he

looks at other girls. When he checks them out or pulls them into his arms on a dance floor. When he leads them up the stairs of our house to his attic room.

Right now, that's how he's looking at me. I can't even breathe, I have completely lost the knowledge and function of how to.

Gannon's hand moves from my hand up to my jaw, where he smooths his thumb over the length of it and clears his throat.

"I hate fighting with you. We go back before skinny jeans were cool. The only two kids who didn't have cell phones in middle school. You're the one who did the cinnamon challenge with me and got me a cool rag when I puked. The one who ran lines with me every day before the seventh grade play. Every second of the day, it's you I want to talk to."

My heart is in my throat, right in the spot where my breath has gone missing. Is he confessing his feelings? Surely, he wouldn't take this moment, in this sweaty, drunken basement, to do that.

"You're my best friend. My family."

And that's where he loses me. Because the minute he says *family*, I'm reminded of what I am to him: A little sister, this immature girl who isn't worthy of dating him. I'm around to be the funny one, the person he can protect and be made to feel like a hero. But I'm not the object of his affection. I never will be. Gannon has never felt that way for me and probably never will.

"You're not my family." I wrench my hand away, springing out of the chair so quickly that the metal legs grind against the concrete of the basement floor.

I hold the tears at bay until I race up the stairs, taking them two at a time to my room. As I jam the key in the lock, my fingers shake with both fury and devastation.

There is no reason that should have gotten my hopes up. I should have stuck to my original plan for tonight. Stay away from Gannon and invite Jameson to run interference. But I didn't. Just like the hundreds of other times, I tried to tell myself that this would be it. The moment he finally notices me. That Gannon would finally come out and say he loves me.

But, of course, it wasn't.

Just when I seem to get over him, to get angry or resigned enough to move on, he reels me back in. When I'm ninety percent of the way to accepting new feelings for someone else, or at least trying to fall for another guy, it's like he has this sixth sense that alerts him to my potential happiness and he has to dash it.

I'm a fish on his line, always there just in case he gets bored. And I allow it.

No more. I can't do this anymore. I can't keep wishing and hoping for some day that will never come.

If I'm ever going to be happy, if I'm ever going to be able to fall in love, I have to cut this out once and for all.

Even if it means losing the one person I love the most.

6

"*I love you*" by Billie Eilish bleeds from the speakers, its haunting melody enchanting my body into a fluid movement that I can't stop.

The lyrics eat at me as my body sways, leaping into a straddle jump and down onto my toe for a vicious, head-spinning turn. How this song describes every feeling I have, of loving someone and having it be completely out of my hands. Of not being able to stop it, even though I hate him. Of not being able to escape the madness.

Some dancers would say this song is too slow, that it has no beat or undertone. I disagree. Its dizzying, hypnotic rhythm lends itself perfectly to the way I want to dance today. Like the world is upside down, and only this floor, my feet, and the music make sense.

I danced from the time I could walk until the end of high school. I was competitive; I'd traverse the state of New York and sometimes the entirety of the East Coast to showcase my routines. But I always danced for myself, especially after my parents' accident.

Aunt Cher was there for every moment my mom and dad

couldn't be, and she'd been an ally, a friend, a teacher, and everything else all rolled into one. She was the one who raised me after my parents died. She's the one I ran home to crying when a girl at my studio was talking shit about me. Looking back, I'm grateful she wanted to give up the life she had to come and raise me. Cher, my mom's younger sister, was an established finance guru in New York City. She was at the top of her game and in peak dating condition, living the life of a single girl in the city when our world came crashing down.

She moved up to Webton, got a work-from-home finance job, and became a mother overnight. We've stumbled a bit along the way, but I love her more than anything on this earth and she returns that love.

Even now, she still lives in Webton, when she doesn't have to so that I have a home to come back to on breaks. I told her I want her to go out and live her own life. She's still so young, could have a family of her own if she wants to. Aunt Cher always looks at me like I'm crazy whenever I say that, and responds, "You're my daughter, you nut."

But when I'd come home from that dance class in tears, she said something that has stuck with me to this day.

Amelie, there are going to be people in this world armed and ready to take you down. You can scream, you can fight them, you can turn everything into a battle. Or you can walk. You can take your pride, your happiness, and your sanity and turn the other way. A lot of people call that chickening out or quitting. You know what I call it? Preserving your joy. If dancing brings you joy, you do it for you. Who the hell cares about medals and being better than the next girl when what you love in the first place is spinning around on that floor. That's what it's about.

It's the mantra I repeat in my head often. A lot of people accuse me of being too nice. Of making the best of even the worst situations. But I think back to Aunt Cher's quote and what getting hurt or upset would do to my joy. It would be the opposite of preserving, that's for sure, which is why I try to live by that motto.

So, I check out studio time with a friend I made in class freshman year and just come in here to destress. I freestyle or put together a short choreography. But dancing? It's for me. I don't need to put it on display. That's when the best kind of dance comes anyway—when no one is watching.

The song trickles off, Billie Eilish almost breaking down at the end in her angelic voice.

"Why don't you try out for the dance team? Honestly, why didn't you freshman year?"

An annoyed tone comes from the door, where Gannon has slipped inside. I didn't even hear him, and I must have had my eyes closed through the final piece of choreography I was making up, because I hadn't seen him in the wall of mirrors in front of me.

Not only has he invaded my space, but suddenly the dance session that had brought me so much joy seemed tainted.

"Because sometimes, you don't do things you love just to be the best at them. I dance because it makes me feel good, because it's not for anyone but me. I don't need medals and ribbons to know how this movement makes me feel. Not all of us need every shred of our business out in the world to feel something."

That was a low blow, but part of me doesn't care. Gannon still cannot grasp why or how some people simply do things just for themselves. Just to be happy internally. I understand, a little bit, why. I know every facet of Gannon's life; I see how he grew up and the ways in which he needed to seek attention.

But he still can't see his own worth, his own internal value. He seeks this validation from strangers because he has no idea how to cope with the gaping hole left by his mother and his absent father.

He chuckles low in his throat, and I can't help the way my gaze falls on the lean muscles of his biceps and how they strain against his gray T-shirt as he crosses his arms.

"I've never seen you so mean, Ams. It's almost refreshing. If it wasn't aimed at me."

My cheeks heat with shame. For years, Gannon has been telling me that I'm too nice, that I should have called out this person or that. Then again, he's also told me it's my best quality. Always with the mixed messages.

This is the one time I don't know how to find the good, which weighs on me heavily. Gannon is my person, and he's been my closest friend for years. Not pushing my upset aside and being able to welcome him home has left me with so much guilt. I'm ashamed that I can't be my cheerful, kind self, especially with him.

Something in me just won't let it go, though.

"I'm not being mean." I pout, because I have no better comeback.

"Ams, you have barely looked me in the eye for weeks. When we were home for the summer, you avoided me like the plague. We need to talk about this."

I let out a sigh. Maybe he's right. Maybe if we talk, at least some of this tension and anger will subside. I know I said I need to cut him out, but I've already had so much loss in my life. If there is a way to salvage anything with Gannon while still pursuing things with Jameson and convincing myself to fall in love with someone else, I have to try.

"Fine. We'll grab poke bowls. Are you free this week?"

The de-constructed sushi bowl restaurant off campus is one of our favorite spots. Gannon always gets extra crab stick in his so he can give it to me, while I let him steal the roe eggs he claims he hates but always mooches out of my bowl.

"Anytime. Always, for you."

He's trying to smooth talk me, but I don't want that. "If we do this, we need to be honest. I don't want TV Gannon. I want the real you."

Something flickers over his face, an expression I've never seen him wear. "I'm as real as I ever am when I'm with you."

That might have been a convincing answer to someone else, but to me, it sounds like a sidestep.

"Thursday, okay?" I decide, needing a few days to prepare.

"We'll leave from the house. I'll drive." He nods.

He always drives, and I always pick the music. It's how we've been doing it since he turned sixteen and got his license. We've spent hours in his car, driving to the lake, to school, up and down the thruway. I miss those times, just the two of us goofing and laughing over songs or stupid jokes we made up as kids.

I give him a terse nod in agreement, and then he turns to go. He knows I'm not to be messed with.

Gannon knows because he knows me better than anyone else does.

Which is both our downfall and our saving grace in this situation.

7

GANNON

Watching her dance is like watching that guy paint the ceiling of the Vatican.

Yeah, so sue me, I don't know what his name is. If I were an art history major, maybe I would. But I'm a marketing major who wants to be TikTok famous. Fine art facts don't really lend themselves to that.

All I know is, as I press my face to the window of the dance studio Amelie is currently occupying, I can't pull my eyes from her body. The way it twists and turns, how she bends and maneuvers like she's swimming through the air gracefully rather than clumsily stumbling like the rest of us.

The song playing over the speakers is a sad fucking melody. The singer croons about love and how fucked up it is, and each lyric is like a bullet in my heart. Don't I know how fucked up love is?

I shouldn't go in, but I do. I interrupt her peace; I push myself on her to have this conversation that she clearly doesn't want to have. We bicker and argue. I'm not used to this with her, we've always had the kind of friendship that everyone envies. A balanced companionship, inside jokes galore, the ability to tell each other the truth.

Well, all except for the most glaring of truths.

I haven't been able to get the image of me hovering inches from her lips in the basement out of my head. It's the closest I've ever gotten to kissing her, not that I haven't stopped myself short on so many occasions over the years. But it was just within reach, the elusive meeting of our mouths that I've tried to keep at bay since I first saw Amelie.

Now, I almost wish I went for it. To see what she tastes like. To confirm that my entire body would relax, that my being would be complete when we were fused.

But I didn't. I can still make out the way her eyes sparkled in the strobe light, the way she was almost egging me on with her breathless panting. I'll never allow myself that slipup again.

When I leave, because Amelie all but dismisses me, my phone starts ringing the second I step outside the arts and theater building.

"Yo," I answer, seeing a familiar name on the screen.

"Some teeth straightening company wants to send you free aligners in exchange for a five-thousand-dollar contract." Quinn snaps her gum directly into the phone, and I have to pull it away from my ear.

"But I already have straight teeth." I'm confused.

"But it's five grand. Can't you fake it?" My sister, the closest sibling in age to me, might as well be saying *uh, duh.*

Quinn, my almost eighteen-year-old sister, actually acts as my manager. Not that the people dealing with her know that. But I'm not going to spend money on outside management, and I'm sure as hell not trusting my business to someone I don't know. Quinn is the shrewdest person I know, and when she graduated high school, she wanted to come with me to Hollywood and work as my agent.

Yes, it would be a learning curve, and yes, so many people would call us idiots for working not only as family, but as inexperienced newbs. I don't care about any of that, though. Ninety percent of the reason I'm pursuing this is to help my family.

Making this money, grabbing this fifteen minutes of fame, it's not just about me. I have five brothers and sisters at home. Yes, my mom got a hefty settlement when my stepdad died, but that was years ago. We've lived okay, decently enough. Our house in Webton is older, not updated, and Mom is slow on getting fixes to things like broken pipes or malfunctioning sockets. She won't address her financials with me, even though I'm basically the other parent to her kids and have been since my sister was born.

But I have to know if she's running dry. I have a feeling she is. Last time I went home, Mallory, the third oldest in our line of half-siblings, told me that Mom didn't have enough money to give her to purchase a yearbook from school. That's when I knew something was up.

Not only has Mom been living off the money from Lyle's will for years, but she also spends way too much. She has a job, one that, now that I'm older and think about it, probably barely covers the mortgage. Then the trips she'd go on and leave me in charge, the online gambling habit that I probably only knew the half of.

If I sign some bigger brand deals, get on another show, or pursue my dream of nabbing some modeling or movie contracts, I can help my brothers and sisters in the way they've always needed to be cared for. Not half-assed, semi-love. I can set them up with the college funds my mom never bothered with. I can make sure they're housed and fed and clean because I know from my childhood before they were around what it feels like not to be.

So people can judge me all they want for taking every oppor-

tunity pitched at me. Promote a weight-loss tea? I'm in. Need
someone for your Halloween catalog to model costumes? Sign
me up. Want a trashy reality TV villain? Great, I'm your guy.
Because those people, the ones judging me, have no idea what
it's like to be in my shoes. And until they do, I don't really give a
fuck about their opinion.

"That's one I don't really think I can fake, sis." I chuckle.
"They'll see my straight teeth in the first Instagram story."

"Yeah, I guess you're right." Quinn blows out a frustrated
breath. "I just want bigger sharks."

Not only is my sister shrewd, but she's good at this. She
wanted to go out and work for me, bring in bigger deals and
even some projects that I dreamed of, not just accepted for
money.

"Any producers in my email?" I ask hopefully.

So the fifteen minutes is good for money, and I'd do it
regardless, but I have always been interested in acting. I starred
in the high school plays even when no one thought it was cool
anymore. I genuinely enjoy acting, and it's another way I can
hide myself. If I can train myself to blend in, to use my charm,
then I'll outwit them all.

"There was something about an upcoming pilot, but the
audition is in Los Angeles in two weeks and I'm not sure ..."

I have class. "Yeah, fuck. It's going to be tough to book
anything."

Booking something would mean being in LA full time and
running myself ragged going to casting calls and auditions. I'm
not sure I'm ready for it, and I want my degree. I can go another
year, finish my undergrad degree at Talcott, and live off the
money I make from Instagram sponsorships. I can still supple-
ment my family that way, too.

As I walk across campus on the phone with my sister, I spot

Callum. He's sitting on a bench outside the library, and he looks fucking *rough*.

"Hey, Quinn? I'm going to call you back tonight. Pass on the aligners thing. Say yes to that sunglasses one you emailed me yesterday. I'll do the ad images and videos this weekend and send them for approval."

Before she can respond, I hang up. It's nothing new, our short and business-like conversations. My sister knows I love her, just like I know she loves me. But when you grow up in a house where no one says that sort of thing, you never admit it.

"Cal," I call out in a friendly tone.

We've been friends ever since he started dating Bevan our freshman year of high school. We were always the two dudes around the three girls, so it was inevitable we'd chill together. But I haven't seen him since I got back to Talcott. We hung once during the summer in Webton, but he was basically a recluse. He's heartbroken and can't seem to get his shit together. I don't blame him.

Callum is staring at the pavement and doesn't even register that I just called out to him. As I approach, I see he's stuck in a daze, completely oblivious to the world going on around him.

I snap my fingers in his face. "Cal, bro, what's up?"

He rears back as if life isn't happening, and he's just ignored it for weeks. "Fuck, what're you doing?"

"I called your name from right over there." I point to the spot not far away.

Callum shakes his head, trying to clear it. "Sorry, I ... I've been out of it."

Sitting down next to him on the bench, I set my backpack at my feet. "Man, you don't have to apologize. I can't say I know how you're feeling, I've never been heartbroken like that. But knowing you and Bevan, I'm hurting for both of you."

The guy looks utterly lost. It's no secret that out of the two,

Bevan was the toxic one. Sure, Callum does dumb shit and has a jealousy complex as big as a planet, but Bev is the one who fucks shit up for them. Her father left her mother in the worst of ways, and she's never gotten over it. Takes out all her daddy issues on Callum, who blindly loves the girl no matter how much she's hurt him over the years. He'd take a bullet for her, even if she was in the process of calling him a scumbag and claiming he never loved her.

"I just don't understand. Why can't something work if two people want it to so badly?" He isn't really asking me, but the universe, if I had to guess.

His question hits home, though. Why can't I just love Amelie? Why can't it just be easy? why can't I just tell her the truth?

But emotions, love, relationships … they're never that easy. We've been complicated from the start, and like always, I just know she deserves someone better than me.

"I don't know," I mumble.

"Never fucking fall in love, man." He shakes his head, an action he can't seem to stop doing.

I don't plan on it. I've only ever seen it destroy people and leave the ones they really care about in the dust.

But maybe if I can achieve fame, I won't have to worry about not falling in love. I won't need it, because everyone will love me. Romantic love, the kind between two people? That never lasts. I've seen it time and again.

But make the world fall in love with you? Yeah, you're set for life. Sure, a scandal or two will make them rail against you. But the public forgives quickly, especially the biggest stars. Look at Brad Pitt. Or Tiger Woods. Hell, even Lance Armstrong had a comeback in some people's books.

Infamy, that kind of love is one I could get down with.

8

"Can you help me check out this book?"

A familiar voice is at my back as I scroll through my computer. I turn, surveying the librarian's desk, and see Jameson.

"Hey." My face splits into a grin.

It's been almost five days since we've seen each other. He's reached out a couple times to talk over text, we grabbed coffee very quickly before class, and he's tried to set up a date. But I've put up excuses or distanced myself every time. With everything swirling around in my head about Gannon, I don't want to set expectations or cloud my mind when I'm with Jameson.

And if I'm honest, I haven't really thought about him. That's bad, right? Now that he's in front of me, I find that my heart is happy. But I don't ache for him. I don't crave talking to him or wake up in the middle of the night swearing that I felt his hands on my body in my dreams.

Maybe that's the kind of love I shouldn't be into. Maybe the easy, simple route is how it is when people decide to spend their life with someone. All married people can't feel that deep, intense connection. Right?

"Thought I'd come visit you at work. Is it creepy that I know I can find you here certain nights of the week?" He grimaces like he just disclosed too much information.

I shake my head, chuckling. "Not at all. I think it's sweet you remember my schedule."

Jameson leans against the desk, a genuine smile on his face. It's nice, an honest expression. There is nothing teasing, egotistical, flirty, or otherwise about his smile. It's just a happy smile.

What the hell is wrong with me, then, that my heart aches for just a little naughty in his tone? For him to do something off-character or sarcastic?

There has got to be something wrong with my head to rebuff this perfect male specimen. To wish he had flaws and a temper and cockiness running within his veins.

Mentally, I slap myself. *Get it together, Amelie.* There is a cute boy in front of me, flirting with me, and he's actually really nice and good in bed. I need to jump on this—no pun intended.

"Has it been busy tonight?" Jameson asks.

I shrug. "Not crazy. I mean, it's a Thursday, which is a big night out, obviously. There are a couple people milling around, a bigger study group on the third floor, and I almost had to kick a group of freshman out."

"Flirting instead of studying?" he asks this as if he knows from experience.

I roll my eyes. "I have no clue why they come to the library to fraternize. It's like, you all have dorm rooms or common rooms you could do that in."

"There is something impressive about the library. You get to show off your brain, brag about your major. Can't say I didn't do it our freshman year. Hoarding around in groups in here, trying to get girls to notice how hard I studied or trying to 'tutor' them. Plus, there is the whole 'in the stacks' thing. You know, having sex in them. Ever catch anyone doing that, as an employee? Ever done it yourself?"

My cheeks heat. I know Jameson is only teasing, but it's the most scandalous flirting he's done with me in the past few weeks since we've been at school.

It hits me that it's kind of weird he's been inside me, and I'm not even sure if I like him. I've never been overly conservative about sex, but with Jameson, it just kind of happened, so it has become the norm when we hang out. But we're not committed, and we barely talk about making this more than casual. God, love lives are so hard.

"I've never ... um ..." I cough awkwardly, and he leans in further.

"Me neither. But it's something I wouldn't mind checking off a bucket list." Jameson winks.

He actually winks. I'm stunned. He's never been this forward. Maybe he's turning on the charm because I haven't been as responsive to him. But either way, this side of him is intriguing. Would I object if he took me by the hand and led me back to the stacks? Pushed me up against a bunch of old books while people were studying and perusing the shelves all around us. Kissed me in hushed nips with silent hands all over my body ...

Well, yes. Because I'd never do that during my shift. But if I was off the clock? I can't say my thighs don't twitch with desire, that I'm not slick in my underwear. It's probably my biggest fantasy. I mean, having sex is great. But having sex pushed up against a bookshelf, surrounded by my favorite stories while passion pours from my soul? Yeah, that sounds like something I'd like to check off, too.

"You're trouble today." I smirk.

"I've missed seeing you. You look pretty, by the way." Jameson sets his book down on the counter.

I blush, but don't acknowledge the compliment or statement.

"*Anatomy and the Vertebrae.* Sounds exhilarating." The joke is followed by a chuckle as I scan it across the library counter, the barcode picked up on my computer and filed under Jameson's name as he swipes his ID.

"It's what gets me going." He winks again, and I think I like this side of him, the one I've rarely seen.

Jameson is a biology major and plans on going into medicine. He says that he's leaning toward anesthesia, so this spine book makes sense. Not that I'd understand any of the jargon, but I appreciate how academic he is. Any guy handling books is like my wet dream.

Books have been my companion since I was a little girl. Yes, I've almost always had Bevan and Taya, but I'm an only child. When you have no one to play with at home, you turn to some kind of escape. Stories were mine. I'd get lost in them, imagine myself in other worlds as other people. When I started suggesting books to friends or the little family I had, and they loved my recommendation, I would get the biggest hit of satisfaction.

I prefer fiction, of any kind. Paranormal, thriller, romance, women's fiction, sci-fi. You name it, I'll read it. Or, I probably already have. The girls like to tease me, because there is always a book or five under the covers of my bed. My room is littered with stacks of books, and Aunt Cher bought a Kindle a while back because she feared for my back with all the books I'd carry around in my bags.

Those stories took me out of my own life when my parents died. They were an escape. If I can bring just one person joy from a book, my life's work will be done. That's why I want to be a librarian. That's why I'm aiming for the highest library in the land.

"Personally, it's Jodi Picoult or Gillian Flynn for me." I grin, leaning my arms on the counter so that we're inches apart.

"What do those authors write about?"

I tap a finger to my chin, trying to sum it up. "Usually heavy topics, like sadness, death, and murder."

Jameson booms out a laugh. "Wow, not the answer I expected from you. Amelie, you continue to surprise me."

"Is that good?" I flirt back, adding a few blinks of my eyelashes.

"Definitely." His fingers toy with mine where they meet on the counter. "So, you going to let me take you on a real date? Come on, surprise me, Amelie. Let's give this a shot."

It's just at this moment that I realize how much I've been missing out on. I've never seen this side of Jameson because I haven't given him a chance. We've hung out, we've had sex, but I've been ruling him out in my head. I've overlooked him, and any other guy, and how they could give me butterflies. Possibly even on the level that Gannon always has.

Because right now, I'm definitely getting an intense fluttering from Jameson.

"Yeah, I think I will. You name the time and place, I'll be there."

He raps his fist on the counter twice, as if he's just closed a deal he's been angling for weeks. It's cute seeing him so confident, and I think Jameson is about to start surprising me.

"I'll pick you up," he promises, and laces his hand in mine before squeezing, then walks off with his book.

God, is there anything hotter than a man walking around with an armful of books? I think not.

So now I have two meetups with two men this week. One, to put an end to things. And the other, to hopefully start anew.

I just hope my heart cooperates in the process.

9

AMELIE

The day has come for my face-to-face with Gannon, and my stomach is in complete knots as I walk to his car.

Eating a poke bowl? It's never going to happen. I just know I'll sit there pushing the food around the paper container, but at least we'll be in public. Not only will that make it less likely that I'll cry, but Gannon can't yell either.

Not that I think he'll yell. The only other time we've gotten into a shouting match was when he started dating Stacy Kepler in high school. The girl who had pantsed me in gym sophomore year and I'd had a maxi-pad on. That fight between Gannon and I ended in us not speaking for three weeks—the longest we've ever gone.

Well, until now, I guess. So I could see how this could go south. But hopefully, I can keep my wits and shove all the real emotions down to make way for our friendship again.

Gannon texted me from the car three minutes ago, and I made my way down to the driveway. Now I stand here, watching his fingers fly over the screen of his cell as he sits in the driver's seat. Dread fills me, but I steel my nerves and wipe my hands on my shorts. I wore my favorite pair of dark wash, cut-off mom jeans paired with a pale pink tank top with bold gray lines striped horizontally. My hair is down in loose waves, and I wore a touch of mascara and my favorite bright pink lipstick.

I feel fun, flirty, and comfortable. I know for a fact my ass looks incredible in these. I'm not going for an "I want you to notice me and drool look," but ever since Gannon couldn't seem to stop looking at me the other night at the party, I can't help but seek that attention again.

"*Watermelon Sugar*" is playing as I duck into the car and I blush furiously. He did this on purpose, to get a rise out of me, and I won't give him the satisfaction.

Matter-of-factly, I disconnect Gannon's phone from the Bluetooth without a word and hook mine up. Rihanna's "*Desperado*" flows over the speakers; the beat one of my favorite to dance to.

Gannon bobs his head as he backs out of the driveway, one hand on the wheel and the other arm slung over the back of my passenger seat as he twists his neck. Both arms bulge as they strain, and why the hell is there something so sexy about the way a man handles a car one-handed? It's almost as if his fist was wrapping around something else, twisting, tugging ...

The heat in my cheeks only intensifies, and I have to look out my window to get myself to calm down. This "friend date" is definitely going to be harder than I thought, and I already thought it impossible.

"Remember the time we jumped into the lake on March first?" Gannon doesn't look at me, instead keeping his eyes trained on the road.

"That's the first thing you're going to say?" I have to laugh because it's so like him.

He plows right over my question. "It was fucking freezing, but you kept talking about new beginnings and shedding our old skins. So I suggested we jump into the water. And you were dumb enough to do it with me. We almost got frostbite."

I chuckle. "I couldn't feel my toes for days."

"Then after, Aunt Cher wrapped us up in blankets and made us hot chocolate. I always loved spending days at your house."

"She told me she missed you when we talked on the phone yesterday." My aunt has always been a sucker for Gannon.

I think she kind of sees him the same way she sees me, as a person to care for who has no one else to care for them. I don't mean it in a negative way, but even with his bustling house, it's always felt like Gannon was alone. Like he has no one looking out for his well-being.

"I miss Cherry, too." He grins, using his nickname for her.

Gannon is a nickname guy. If you got one, it means you're special. I used to put stock into the fact that I was one of the first people in Webton he nicknamed.

"Anyway," he continues, "this can kind of be like our March first. Shedding the hurt, starting anew with each other."

Ah, now it dawns on me why he's using this analogy. Gannon isn't great when it comes to talking about his feelings, but he's trying for me. That melts some of the ice on my heart and my pride.

"Yeah." I swallow. "I think it could."

He pulls up in front of the poke bowl place a few minutes later, and we get out.

"Hey, Tran." Gannon waves to the owner, who has seen us here many times over our three years at Talcott.

"You came back! I haven't seen you two in a while." She smiles jovially, sincerely happy that we're back to eat at her restaurant. "Wait! I watched you on TV! Oh man, you almost won."

Tran starts to laugh, and Gannon lights up. I can see how ecstatic he is when he gets recognized, and it clicks that I haven't been around him enough since he left the show to see this. I've had one or two girls approach me when I've been working at the library to try and suss out whether I'd introduce them, but other than that, I haven't been privy to his fanfare.

As he walks over to autograph a dollar Tran has pulled from the cash register, I stand there and watch as two other people come up and start asking him about the show. Now I'm kind of glad I've kept my distance. I can't imagine how jealous I'd be if we were walking through campus with the number of people I'm sure stop him every five seconds.

I'd be reminded all over again of how he betrayed me. Not that it's really betrayal, when he knows nothing of the feelings I've always harbored for him.

Annoyance needles at me as I stomp to the register. "Um, can we place our orders?"

Gannon looks at me like I've lost my mind. I've never been this rude in my entire life. It makes me take a step back and cover my mouth as shame floods my stomach.

"I'm so sorry. Would we be able to order now? I think ... I'm just hungry, I think."

Gannon's jaw is still on the floor as Tran nods slowly and begins to jot down what we want in our bowls.

"Where is my Ams and what have you done with her?" Gannon asks as we take a seat at a table by the front windows.

His Ams. I hate that my heart calls out to him when he says it like that.

I scowl, both at my heart and at him. "I'm not yours. And I just don't like when people go all celebrity on you. About the show."

"Why are you so pissed off about the show? Let's get this elephant out of the way, because I feel like it's where all of our problems are coming from. You were happy when I got it." He looks utterly confused.

Either he's a better actor than I thought, or he really has no clue how I feel about him. Either way, I was not happy when he got the show. I plastered on the fakest of smiles, because I knew how excited he was, and went to my room after to cry into my pillow.

"I just ... I didn't like who I saw on my television screen. That's not you, Gannon. And ..."

How am I supposed to tell him that it cut me to the core?

"That's all." I shrug, too chickenshit to admit all of the other stuff.

He reaches across the table and holds my hand. Before he can explain, because his gorgeous mouth is hanging open like he wants to, Tran sets our bowls down in front of us. Usually, my mouth would water at all of the fresh fish and vegetables. Today? I can barely look at it.

Gannon hops right back into the conversation when she leaves. "Ams, it's show business. The producers tell us half the things to say. I never really felt that way about her."

Somehow, that makes this all the more worse.

Gannon continues. "This was my foot in the door. I like the TV things, I enjoy acting and being in front of people. I could see it really becoming a career. But it's also a concrete way to immediately provide for my family. You know, more than anyone, how much they rely on me."

I do know that. Gannon's mom was a special breed of parent. You could tell she cared but was so apathetic sometimes. She'd leave for days on end, then come home showering her kids with love and presents. Gannon and his siblings weren't necessarily hurting, but they did live in the poorer section of Webton. And often, Gannon would have to go without lunch in high school so his brothers and sisters could afford to eat. I'd always make an extra sandwich and bring it with me, just in case.

"I'm sorry I came across as fake, but it kind of was. The audience, the contestants, the people who follow me on social media, they don't know the real me. You do. Our friends do. I don't want to be my real self on TV, with those people, because I save that for you."

Well, shit. Now my heart is a melted pool on the tile floor of this restaurant. He saves that for *me*.

I can't stop thinking about the way he looked at me in the basement. He was about to kiss me, I could feel it. That moment gave me hope, lit anew the flame that had always burned for him in my chest. It was confirmation that maybe I wasn't crazy, that maybe he did feel the same way about me.

"Why do you save that just for me?" I almost whisper this.

It's the first time I've ever tried to bring this up, to question even a little bit about the way we might be more than just friends.

He squeezes our connected hands. "Because you're my best friend."

I might have that hope, but it's clear, no matter what I thought I'd seen, that Gannon is never going to act on it.

"Forgive me? I miss you." He turns up that smile to the megawatt one I can never refuse.

My options are limited. There are only two, and only one that keeps him in my life. Telling him the truth and that I'm in love with him isn't even on the table if he can't answer why he saves that side of himself for me. So I can either walk away, not taking his friendship as enough for me, or I can push everything down, like I've always done, and keep this relationship. Right now, I can't imagine my life without Gannon in it, even with all of the hurt and anger he's brought.

I've lost too many people close to me. I'm not willing to do that again.

So, I force myself to smile. "Oh, fine. But you owe me a six-pack of—"

"Your favorite white cranberry seltzer? Already on it." He grins.

"Of course you are." I shake my head and poke a fleshy piece of salmon with my fork.

We eat in silence for a moment, and I have to admit I'm happy we're going to go back to normal. *Ish.*

Gannon stretches back, a sliver of perfect abs peeking out when his T-shirt rises with the motion. "So, should we go see that new scary movie this week? The one where she murders her whole family because the devil is inside her? Let's go on Tuesday. I'll buy you Skittles."

My favorite movie treat. He'd get a large popcorn and a Dr. Pepper, and we'd both steal each other's. His arm would rest right next to mine. How many times have I wished, in the darkness of a theater, that he'd lace his fingers through mine?

How quickly he can shift from our months-long fight to right back into our routine. We're besties again, right? That's what I told him? My heart sinks a little.

"I have a date with Jameson that night," I tell him.

I divulge that because it's true, but also because I want to make it apparent to Gannon. Both, because he needs to know there will be another man in my life, and if I'm being honest, because I want just one more attempt to make him admit any feelings to me.

Jameson texted me last night asking if I wanted to go for beers and bowling, and I agreed.

"Hmm." Gannon makes a non-committal but annoyed noise.

My heart beats one hard thump against my rib cage. I can no longer allow him to influence my love life. This is a place I need to grow from, and Gannon's opinion is no longer welcome.

"Stop it. He's a nice guy and as my"—I gulp—"friend, I want you to like him. To get used to him coming around with me."

Amber eyes burn in my direction. "No guy will ever be good enough for you."

My stomach is at my feet. I can't take this anymore. So I

decide I won't. "New rule, since we're starting anew. You are no longer allowed to make judgments, suggestions, or decrees about my love life."

"But—" he starts to argue.

I hold up a hand. "No, Gannon. I can't hear that stuff."

I leave out the part about getting my hopes up that he feels a type of way about me every time he puts another guy down.

"Fine." He waves me off, and everything we just accomplished seems to be stilted now.

Our drive home is okay, with both of us making small talk about everything and nothing at all. But there is still an elephant that sits between us, one that will never be resolved because we both refuse to acknowledge it.

10

J asmine glides in front of me, her straight, silky hair in a shade of ink swishing around her body.

My eyes lock on her, and I try to force them to stay there and not rove around the room looking for someone else. After all, I have a fucking model grinding on my dick. That should make this party epic for so many reasons.

Jasmine and I met at a *Mrs. Right* sponsored party in Los Angeles. She's one of the up-and-coming models in the industry, and we clicked while talking about the kind of tequila she prefers. Her mother is from Mexico, and she schooled me the entire night on the right way to lick, slam, and suck ... literally. After that, we went back to her hotel room and had a lot of fun.

When she texted last week and asked if she could see me, I didn't exactly feel like getting on a plane. And what better way to party than at college. Sure, she's used to insider parties and velvet-roped clubs, but Talcott is a fucking blast, and I could show her a good time. Plus, it would mean having a distraction if Amelie invited Jameson to our party tonight.

"You look so fucking hot tonight," Jasmine whispers in my ear, biting the lobe.

My cock should be hard as stone right now, any heterosexual, red-blooded male's would be, but I feel nothing.

"So do you." I grab her hips, trying to make myself get into it.

The dance floor in the living room of our Prospect Street house is packed, per usual, and I know about ten percent of the faces. But they all know mine. My name has been shouted no less than a dozen times in the last five minutes, and people have been trying to snap photos of Jasmine all night.

She's lapping it up. At first, she'd fought back about coming to Talcott, saying it was beneath her. Yes, she really said that. But now she's all over the attention, posing for photos when frat guys come up to Instagram story with her.

Did I do this to fuck with Amelie? Absolutely. Am I licking my wounds that we made up and she turned around and whacked me with the two-by-four that she was going on an official date with Jameson? Yes. Do I really want to hang out with this model over trying to seduce Amelie, something I only think about in my wildest dreams?

Abso-fucking-lutely not.

But that fuckwad is here, cuddled up on the couch with her in the living room, bringing her drinks. And I couldn't face another night having to be her *friend* while he got to take her upstairs at the end of the party.

I make out Amelie's face through the crowd, right as Jasmine bends over to drop it low on my crotch.

Hazel eyes flick to my date, then back up to match my gaze. She raises an eyebrow, as if to say, *classy*.

Poison singes my veins. Seriously? She has the balls to make a comment, albeit silent body language, about my date? She's sitting on that asshat's lap when she knows how I feel about him, but apparently, making sweeping judgments about who is touching me tonight.

I'm not used to this Amelie at all. My best friend is usually the quiet, kind type. She doesn't tell people what she's really thinking so as not to offend them. It's like the world has flipped upside down since I came back from filming *Mrs. Right*.

"Do you have any pills?" Jasmine coos at me. "I want to get wild."

I have to refrain from wrinkling my nose in disgust. I'm not an idiot when it comes to the drugs that are done both at my college and in Hollywood. It's not a normal night at Talcott if someone isn't doing lines in the bathroom. But I've just never been into that sort of thing. Alcohol gets me fucked up enough. I don't need to use to have a good time.

"No." My voice sounds absent, even as she's practically mounting me on the dance floor.

I watch as Amelie speed walks across the room, into the open foyer, and up the stairs.

Where is she going?

"I'll be right back," I'm telling the girl who only came here for me before I can think better of it.

Jasmine protests at my back, but I don't stop. Amelie is out of sight before I can catch where she's gone upstairs. Is she in her room, waiting for Jameson? In the bathroom? Is it creepy if I wait around?

As if answering my question, I hear the toilet flush and Amelie comes walking out. She does a double take at me standing in the hallway, and I go in right away. Call it anger fueled by alcohol, but something still hasn't been sitting right about our conversation the other day.

"So you're going to sit on his lap and give me the judgy eyes?" I snarl.

Shit, I'm in a real mood tonight. Who knew? It was looking at her with him, having to watch them this past week, that got me to this point. And my own stupid inability to just admit to her that I've been in love with her from the moment I saw her in the fifth grade.

"That's rich, coming from you." She snorts, and I can't help the way my eyes track down the light purple dress hugging her curves.

"What's that supposed to mean?" I bite back, fisting my hands so that I don't reach out and touch her.

"Next time you decide to bring whores to the house, just let the rest of us know, would you?" Venom drips from her tongue, past those swollen, glistening lips.

She looks like she's been kissing someone, the skin of her mouth a shade of blood red, and fury does not begin to describe the thing that begins to pulse through my veins. I'm fucking tired of hearing her moan for another man. I'm fucking livid that he gets to see her like that.

It's been a week of her going on and on about Jameson, of him hanging around the house and sleeping in her bed.

I'm out of my mind with jealousy, and that isn't me.

"What was that rule you threw at me? No judging, talking about, or suggesting things about your love life? Well, I'm calling bullshit if I'm not afforded the same."

Amelie rolls her eyes, and I want to slam my mouth onto hers just for that cheeky movement. "That was when it comes to actual relationships, Gannon. Not Instagram THOTs who only flew here to take pictures with you and post on TikTok."

"Where is that clown anyway? He just off doing whatever while you're walking around alone?" It sounds so immature, but I can't help myself.

She glowers at me. "Jameson had to leave early. He has an exam to study for tomorrow."

"The guy you're dating shouldn't ever leave you. If that were me ..."

I falter, realizing what I just said. Amelie takes a step forward, seeing if I'll go on.

I know everything Amelie wasn't saying in our talk the other day. She's not just upset with me because I turned into a different person on TV. She's heartbroken from what I said to Cassandra on *Mrs. Right*. I told another girl, one I barely knew, that I was in love with her and wanted to marry her. Not only did I mean none of it, but I swore a long time ago, probably in front of Amelie, that I would never fall in love.

I know how Amelie feels about me. What I said to Cassandra probably devastated her. But she wasn't brave enough to bring it up in our talk, not that I'd ever given her any inkling that I'd be receptive to it. This is as much her fault as it is mine. We're both harboring secrets that prevent us from being our normal selves.

Or had we ever really been that way to begin with? Maybe as kids, forming a friendship all the way back when. But we hit puberty, and both of us probably started to form an attraction. My solution was to hide it completely, while Amelie has looked at me with those hopeful eyes for years.

"What was that? If you were what, Gannon? If you were ..." She's challenging me.

I dangle there, my breathing completely off. Is this the moment? The one where we finally stop bullshitting each other?

"Never mind. He's a chump, that's all."

Amelie snorts, turning to walk away but then whirling back around. "Of course, you won't say anything. Of course, you'll mask whatever it was that you were actually going to say, and use some slang and hurl it at him. At least he isn't a coward who can't admit what he's feeling."

She turns on her heel to scamper away.

"Oh no, you fucking don't." I reach out to grab her elbow, because hell no, is she walking off.

I'm done with this. All of it.

But the minute my fingertips graze her skin, she comes around swinging. Just like the time I walked into the living room at the end of last year and she rounded on me.

Luckily, this time, I swerve out of the way of her small fist and then straighten. The shock in Amelie's eyes is clear as day, and so is the fire. The hurt. The fury. There are so many things swirling in those amber pools that they all hit me like a bullet straight in the middle of my chest. Those emotions sting more than a punch from her ever could.

Before I can blink, she's launching herself at me. And I catch her, as if knowing that's exactly what she was about to do. Like we're on the same brainwave.

One minute we're arguing, screaming at each other in the second-floor hallway. And the next, we're backing into her bedroom, knocking glass lamps to the floor and pulling curtains down. We're a whirlwind, a tornado out of control and not responsible for anything that happens from this point forward.

The kiss that started when she jumped into my arms hasn't stopped, and I'm giving her eleven years of pent-up sexual frustration. My tongue fucks her mouth roughly, our teeth clashing, but nothing stopping us from feasting.

I'm not sure how we're moving so fluidly in relation to each other's bodies, though, when each collision with an inanimate object ends in destruction. But we are. She pulls my shirt off; I shimmy the hem of her dress to her hips. My belt comes undone. Her panties are torn away.

The next thing I know, I'm lifting her onto her desk, the wood shaking under the intensity of our movements. Amelie wraps her legs around my waist. I unbutton my fly and push my boxers down.

There is no conversation, no agreement or disagreement. Every action has been leading to this, and neither of us will speak for fear that it will end.

I pause for a fraction of a second to look into her eyes, and her hands pull where they're fisted in my hair. A silent plea, not to stop, to keep going, because we both need this. Want this. Crave it from the depths of our fucking souls.

My cock pushes into her slick wetness, and then I thrust in to the hilt.

"Fuck!" I shout, though no one can hear me.

The noise that comes from Amelie's lips is the best fucking sound I've ever heard in my life. A mix between this breathy little moan and a raspy squeal, I could eat it up for the rest of my life. I'd starve myself for a decade if I knew that sound was at the end.

Jesus Christ, this is a dream. It has to be. Because as I'm pounding into her, the veins in my cock expanding with every movement of my hips, I sincerely can't believe it's happening. Amelie writhes against me, and we're matching each other. Her pussy drips at the entrance, and I know I'll never get the smell of her out of my memory.

One of the straps holding her dress up slips from her shoulder, and I'm a savage. I rip it all the way down. Her dress is bunched at her torso, and I finally, *finally*, get to touch the tits I've been having wet dreams about since I was twelve. They bounce in my hands as I fuck her, and when I roll one nipple, she arches backward so that the crown of her head is almost touching the desk. It's the hottest thing I've ever seen in my life.

We may only have been fucking for minutes, but it feels like I've been inside her for years. Like it's destiny that brought us to this place. That sounds corny, but the atmosphere in her darkened room is other-worldly. I can't describe it. The sense that this is the most important moment of my life looms so large over my head.

I'm so close to coming, I nearly blurt out things I should never say to my best friend. That I'm in love with her. That I want to do this over and over again. That I want to marry her and make a family.

Shit I have no business promising anyone, especially her.

"Oh. My. God." Amelie's head snaps forward, her body cradling into mine, and she moans so loudly into my ear that it's tattooed in my canal forever.

Her breaths come in puffs, and I take sick, wicked pleasure in the fact that I'm making her come all over my dick. I want to push her back, to see the look on her face when she does it, but that almost feels too intimate. I'm inside her, but I have no idea how this will go next. If I see that look on her face when she falls apart, I'll never be able to stop craving her.

Even with all the thoughts rushing through my head like an avalanche, my spine stiffens with my impending climax. I hold Amelie tight, all of the breath in my lungs ceasing to exist.

When I come, it feels like my world completely centers. Like it's been off its axis this entire time, my whole life, and now I can finally exit in an upright state.

I have to clamp my lips together as I come down from the high, worried I'll start telling her all of the things I've locked away for a decade.

Oh, crap.

Double, double crap.

"You came in me." The words come out of my mouth like a half-statement, half-question.

Gannon clearly is still lost in the haze of our passion because he doesn't even register the question. Instead, he's framing my face with his hands and pressing his lips to mine. I get lost in the kiss as his tongue sweeps into my mouth, our bodies still connected with him inside me.

The wetness from our orgasms soaks me, but I can barely seem to care. It's only when something smashes below us, a partygoer probably causing damage, that I'm aware of our surroundings.

"Gannon ... a condom. We didn't use a condom." I try to shake away the cobwebs he planted in my brain.

As if coming back to reality, he stops kissing me and blinks once. Then twice. Then he pulls out and says, "Fuck. Fuck, *fuck*."

His half-hard cock bobs in the air, and I can't stop looking at it. Christ, he's huge. All this time I've wondered, and the first shot I get to truly look at him is in my dark bedroom while I'm drunk. What a shame. A body like Gannon's deserves more appreciation.

"It's okay, I'm on the pill. We can get Plan B just to be safe," I try to assure him and to calm my own nerves.

I'm not sure what to do now, as I sit on my desk where we just screwed each other's brains out. But Gannon, he clearly knows what to do. He's pacing around the room, muttering to himself as he pulls all his clothes back on and tucks his cock into his pants.

"I have to go back downstairs." He turns to me, his eyes burning with some expression I can't read.

Surprise sweeps through me like a wind gust I wasn't expecting. "Oh, um, okay?"

Part of me expected him to carry me over to my bed, to undress me slowly while we whispered and talked into the night. I've dreamed of this moment, of having sex with Gannon, for so long. I've thought out every detail. I've tried to imagine the way it would feel to fall asleep in his arms. I, at least, thought that he would be courteous enough to talk out whatever the hell just happened.

Apparently, we'll be having none of that.

"It's just ... Jasmine. You know?" He shrugs.

Hearing her name drop out of his mouth exactly one minute after his cock was inside me is equal to taking a bullet. I actually flinch, pressing the heel of my hand to my heart because of the pain he just shot me with.

It's worse than the pain I felt when I walked down the stairs earlier in the night and saw her draped all over him on the dance floor. I have no idea when she arrived, but I noticed her. It would be impossible not to. Her knockout body graces half the paid ads on my social media channels. To know that we had that talk about our friendship, and then to see him turn right around and invite a girl here.

It hurts like hell. Knowing that she's top of his mind when he just did me on my desk is a form of torture I never want to experience again.

"I see." I cluck my tongue, my arms wrapping around myself.

Suddenly, I feel so exposed that I want to bolt. How stupid could I be? This wasn't anything more than a heat of the moment thing, a way for Gannon to get off because he felt like it. This wasn't going to be the culmination of years of friendship turning romantic. This was a quick fuck. What just happened wasn't the dive into love I'd been certain was coming since I was ten, it was a catapult off a cliff that would simultaneously break my heart and ruin our relationship.

And that has me lashing out. "Actually, I don't. If you wanted to get off, you should have just screwed her."

Thinking about her long, magazine-famous legs wrapped around his waist makes me want to hurl. Gannon opens his mouth. Shuts it. Opens it back up.

"And if you wanted someone tonight, maybe Jameson should have stuck around." He smacks me back with his words.

Tears spring to the corners of my eyes, and I'm so confused and hurt. "What the hell is wrong with you?"

I can't even pretend to battle him right now. To use my words to stab him back. It's crazy how I went from pure bliss and pleasure one minute to rage and misery the next.

"Amelie, we just had sex while the girl I invited to our house from out of town is downstairs by herself." He waves his hands as if trying to make me see how valid his point is.

Wrenching my underwear back into place and pulling my skirt down, I feel the anger rising in my throat. "Oh, no, by all means, please get back to the perfect model you brought here. Wouldn't want to misinterpret this *fuck* as anything."

It's distinct, the pain when your heart shatters into a million tiny pieces in your chest. I thought I'd felt it before, all those other times I'd pined or cried over Gannon. But no, this one is the motherload. This feels like I could crumple into a ball and just die with how badly the organ in my chest aches.

No point in waiting around to see what he says or if he wants to discuss this. I'm exhausted, broken, and now worried about the possibility of a pregnancy. Just one more mistake I've made when it comes to Gannon Raferty.

When will I ever learn?

I never asked Gannon to get up with me in the morning, but when I walk into the kitchen with my car keys in my hands, he's sitting at the table.

Without a word, he rises, takes my keys from my hands, sets them on the table, and then nods his head toward the door. Ah, I get it. My white knight wants to be the one to drive me to the drug store to buy Plan B so we don't have a baby neither of us is ready for. How classy of him.

Last night has left me numb. Not only does this ruin everything between Gannon and I, ending years of friendship, but I have to tell Jameson about this. I barely slept, but instead, laid in a cold sweat in my bed half the night trying to reconcile what we'd just done.

Those minutes were the best of my entire life. I felt closer to the one person I've always wanted to be with, a dream I never thought would happen. Gannon ripped that all away when he ripped my heart out.

So while I'm recovering from that knife wound in my chest, I'll have to put one in someone else's. Jameson doesn't deserve this. No, we're not technically committed, but our spark was really beginning to burn. We could have been something, and

I've ruined that. I didn't even think about him, not one ounce of guilt, before letting Gannon strip me naked and have his way.

Thinking about having to have this conversation with Jameson, to admit what I've done, makes me sick to my stomach. Or maybe that's the thought that I could be growing a baby right this very minute.

Or that I'm going to take a pill that ensures I will never have Gannon's baby. When it's one of the things I've dreamed about in my wildest fantasies for the future.

"Ams, I freaked out. I'm sorry. You deserve so much better than that. You deserve everything. If I could go back ... fuck, I wish I could go back."

His deep voice penetrates the awkward silence of the car.

"So you could take it back." I nod, a tear dripping onto my lap.

"No! Hell no!" Gannon gets loud, reaching over to put two fingers under my chin so that I have to look at him. "I want to go back so that we did that the way I've always wanted to. With no party downstairs, with no unanswered questions about whether I am serious about you. You deserved candles and music and roses on the bed. I wish I could have explored every inch of you, slowly, so slowly—"

My heart is beating in time to his voice. What is he saying? I'm about to ask when the ringing of my cell phone interrupts us. I shouldn't look, but barely anyone actually calls me. They know I either won't have my phone or won't be checking for calls. So when I see it's my aunt Cher, I know she needs me. She always texts to set up a call to make sure it's a good time.

"Aunt Cher?" I say, the muffled noises in the background of the call sounding a lot like crying.

"Bubs ... I have to tell you something." The tone of her voice conveys all the seriousness in the world.

There are certain times in your life where you'll get a feeling.

This out-of-body, can't believe this is actually happening, type of feeling. I had one of them last night, with Gannon ... though it was in an extremely good way. The other time in my life I've had that feeling is when they told me both my parents were dead.

That second feeling, the earth-shattering, want to die too one, is the one that fills my stomach right now.

"I have cancer."

And just like that, my entire world falls apart.

12

I f you've never experienced what it's like to be completely numb, I both recommend the hell out of it and absolutely don't at the same time.

I've been numb twice in my life—the first, when I was told that my parents were never coming home. And the second, just hours ago when my aunt, the only family left in my life, called to tell me she has stage three ovarian cancer.

My limbs feel like heavy burdens that I'll have to carry for the rest of my life. Extremities cease to exist, my fingertips and cheeks tingling from the lack of feeling in them. The fuzzy din of my brain whirs on and on, latching on to different sounds or ideas but never fully being able to grasp them.

"Ams? *Ams*?" Gannon shakes my arm, his face floating into view.

He looks concerned, but I can't register any feeling of my own to worry about that.

"What can we do? Should we drive you home?" Taya is asking, holding on to one of my hands.

I'm sitting on the couch between Taya and Gannon, and apparently, Bevan is on her way here. I need to move, need to pack, and go home. I need to call Aunt Cher because I'd almost thrown my phone out of a moving car window and into traffic when she told me she has …

Has …

I can't even think the word, much less say it out loud.

But the way I reacted was not what she needed. I need to call her back, to hear it all, to support her. This numbness needs to pass, because I need to be the strong one.

That's what she was for me when my parents died. I could be the numb one. I didn't have to stand up and face anything, to fight, because they were already gone. Aunt Cher was there for me every step of the way, and now she needs me to be her shoulder. The one who lifts her up and takes care of her.

If I could just feel. If I could just *move*.

Mustering everything I have, I stand. It feels like I'm pressing against a ton of bricks to do so. "I have to go home."

The two of them jump up next to me, but Taya speaks. "I'll get your bag packed, don't worry about any of that. Bevan will gas your car—"

"I'm driving her." Gannon's deep tone invades my ears and I wince.

Do you know what's worse than hearing your only family member has cancer? Hearing that news and then having to go into a goddamn CVS to buy a pill that will get rid of any chance of having a baby with your best friend you accidentally had sex with. Not to mention, while said best friend, who may or may not be a friend anymore but definitely doesn't want to be your boyfriend, is with you at the CVS.

Yeah, my life has turned into an utter hellscape.

I can't argue with Gannon, though. There is no one who knows me better, who knows how Aunt Cher and I operate. She loves him just as much as she loves me, and it'll lift her spirits if he shows up in Webton too.

Plus, selfishly, I want to forget everything that has happened in the last twenty-four hours and just lean on him. After all is said and done, he's my person, and you need your person when stuff like this happens.

Taya disappears upstairs, and I just stand in the living room without a clue as to what to do.

Gannon comes into view, and I kind of forgot he was here. How funny that things can change at the drop of a hat. One second, I'm worried about what sleeping with him means, and now it's irrelevant. I have no room in my head for any of that.

"Amelie, I know we have a lot to talk about—" He starts toward me, holding out his arms like he might touch me.

"No." I cut him off and shrug away.

There is no time for any of that now. My sole focus, the only thing I'm required to do from this point forward, is breathe and get my aunt healthy.

"I'm not talking about this. Forget it all. You are my best friend, and I need you." It's definitive.

Whatever he said to me in that car, whatever relationship we would have wrecked or plan we would have concocted, it's done now. I can't look back. There is only forward.

Something passes over Gannon's face. Is it relief that he's off the hook? Something else? I don't have the patience or time to dissect it right now.

He gives a curt nod. "Right."

I give it a beat, expecting him to say more, but he doesn't. Just as I'm about to walk away, he interrupts me.

"Just ... let me ask one thing?"

I don't object, but I don't give him explicit permission.

"The pill ... you're okay, right? Are you feeling okay? I never want you to be in pain, and I'm sorry we had to get that. I was so stupid, and you should never feel like—"

"Gannon, does it seem like I'm okay? This is quite possibly

the most painful moment of my life." And we both know it has nothing to do with the fact that I took the morning after pill.

He shuts right up, smashing his lips together.

And that's it. No more discussion about the moment that upended both our worlds.

But like I said, I can't agonize over that. Forward is the only direction I can go because Aunt Cher needs me.

Her small fingers grip mine tight, and I can feel the jitters in her bones.

Amelie is sheet white, swimming in one of my old high school football sweatshirts as she curls into the passenger seat. She looks so small and helpless like the world might swallow her whole.

It wasn't even a discussion of who would take her home. Bevan and Taya took one look at me and didn't even bother arguing. They knew I'd fight hell and high water to put her in my car and hold her hand as I drove us to Webton.

Taya was the one to come talk to me as I threw a random assortment of clothes in a bag. I had no idea how long we'd be there, but I was prepared to drop out of school if it was what Amelie needed.

"She needs you, Gannon." Taya walks into my attic room and sits down on the couch on the far wall.

I grit my teeth. I'm so tired of people trying to tell me to be a standup guy when I already am. "I know that."

"I'm serious. You cannot think of anything but what Amelie needs. No business calls, no social media, no calling models."

"Do you think I'm that big of an asshole, Tay? Jesus fucking Christ." I whip a sweatshirt into my bag, anger simmering in my veins.

"No, but I think you're a rising influencer who has worked hard for his money and doesn't want to let it slip. No one faults you for that."

Leave it to Taya to see beneath the surface. She might be the quiet one, the one who won't cause any ripples, but she also shoots straight as an arrow.

"I'm one hundred percent focused on Amelie. She is my priority. She is my everything." If only Taya knew how true that was.

"And this one is the most important. No charming her. No making her feel like you're her boyfriend, or that you'll protect her from the world. I may not know what happened at that party, but I can tell something did, and she doesn't need that shit right now. If she feels like she can put all of her trust in you, and then you leave her ... I will kill you with my bare hands."

Fury, hot and passionate, licks up around my neck. I stretch it, trying to escape the flames, because I don't have time to explode on Amelie's best friend.

"You all really think so low of me. You have no idea what I've sacrificed not to give Amelie that idea. So don't start with me. She is the only one I'm focused on, everything else in my life be damned. I don't need a fucking scolding. Get out."

Taya left my room with a weary backward glance. We both knew that I had to skate a thin line, this incredibly razor-thin boundary between being a shoulder to lean on and being the man that Amelie would put all of her faith in. Taya's right, I'm not her boyfriend. And while I wish I could be her everything,

I'm still fully aware of all the reasons I have to keep her at arm's length romantically.

Hell, before she got the call from Aunt Cher, I was certain our friendship and anything we had between us was over. There was a moment there, one where I was about to show Amelie all the sides of myself that I'd hidden.

I was this close to admitting I'm in love with her.

Now I look over at where she sits beside me in the car, and my stomach clenches with how stupid I've been. Just another day in the life of trying to be her best friend but not get too close, and I've fucked it up again.

Because she should be focusing on her aunt and using me as a shoulder to cry on. Except I had to seduce her and now things will be awkward no matter what we do.

Not that I'm not going to try my damnedest to put all of my needs aside.

Though hard as I try, I can't get the night in her bedroom out of my head. I've dreamed about being inside Amelie for so long. A goddamn decade almost, though my ten-year-old self wasn't thinking in as graphic terms as it actually happened.

Having sex with her, hearing her noises, having her look at me with those hooded, lusting eyes ... my world could end right now, and I'd be a happy man. It's the singular best experience of my life.

But when I finished, and reality came slamming back up at me like the ground was swallowing my body ...

I don't know what got into me. I should have never mentioned Jasmine after we just had sex. After I came inside Amelie without a condom. But part of me freaked the fuck out. My brain just went haywire, and I was thinking about what I'd just done to our friendship. I was thinking about what an asshole I was that I invited a girl to the house and took a different one up to a bedroom. I was thinking about how I'd kept my secrets, about how I felt about her for so long, that I couldn't damn well tell her right there and then.

I was thinking about how I'd done it all wrong with Amelie. I'd thought a lot about what our first time together might look like. Half-drunk at a party, on top of a desk, not caring about protection was not the image I'd conjured. Call me a romantic.

I freaked, okay? It was fucking wrong of me, and I know I hurt her worse than I ever could have.

Though now, that hurt is replaced by an even larger wound.

My hand automatically moves to grasp hers as we turn onto the street where she grew up. After Amelie's parents died, her aunt Cher moved into the family house as not to uproot Ams through all the grief.

How many nights have I spent in that two-story colonial, sleeping on the couch so I didn't have to go home? How many movies did we watch sprawled out on the floor with popcorn? How many times did I sneak in her window when my mom didn't come home? How many times did we bake cookies when Amelie was sad about her parents missing out on something?

There are endless memories here, and all of them start and end with the woman who is drowning in sorrow in the seat next to me.

This is my second home, and it feels strange that I suddenly don't want to enter it. Because I know when I do, we're going to have to face the life-threatening illness ahead.

And if I feel this way, I can't imagine how Ams is coping.

"I'm right here." I squeeze her hand as I roll us into park.

"I can't go in." She sits stock-still, her eyes wide and bloodshot.

She needs me to hold her. But I'm not just here for that. I know my job. So I do it.

"Amelie, listen to me." I physically turn her head to make her look at me. "I know you don't want to. No one wants to face something like this. But you need to take five seconds, a deep breath, and then push all of that fear aside. Because Cherry needs you. You don't get to be scared, because you have to absorb all of her feelings so she can focus on fighting. It's going to suck, I know that. But you have to suck it the hell up."

I hear the intake of her breath and then see the way she holds it in her lungs. It comes whooshing out, and then she nods at me.

"Thank you. I needed that smack. Let's go." She squeezes my hand back, and I know that dose of tough love is what she needed.

I know because I know everything about her.

My steps are leaden as we walk to the front door, her duffel and mine slung over both my shoulders. Amelie has a key, so there is no need to knock or ring the doorbell. She unlocks the door and lets us in.

The scent of her childhood home has always been the same; sage and grapefruit. Aunt Cher purchases this one candle by the bundles. I think she has a closet full to the brim of backups because it's her favorite. The warmth of it wraps around me like a hug, comforting but also too familiar.

And there is nothing familiar about this.

"Amelie?" We hear Cher's voice, and since I know the layout of this house like the back of my hand, I can tell she's in the living room.

My hand is on the small of Ams' back after dropping the duffels by the stairs, and our feet hit the shaggy white carpet before my eyes land on her aunt.

"Hi." Cher smiles at her niece, and Amelie flies into her.

They hug tight, Cher half-standing as Amelie stoops down to cling to the only parent she's known for years. I stand respectfully by, letting them have their moment. It dawns on me that I'll have to stay here with them, with Amelie, and try to avoid the conversation of us. I could always go home, I suppose, but dealing with my mother's antics while Amelie needs me is not something I feel like putting up with.

Finally, they break apart, both wiping their eyes. Cher looks around Amelie at me and grins.

"I'm sick, and so, what? You thought bringing a movie star home would help?" She's always busting my chops.

"Cherry." I smile at her, and she opens her arms.

She looks thinner than I've ever seen her, with big blue bruising bags under her eyes. I've called her Cherry since she moved into Amelie's childhood home. Because of her name, but also because she'd always wear this shade of cherry red on her lips.

That color is gone.

When I hug her, I can feel her spine. I bite my tongue to keep from getting choked up, because how the hell do I know what to do in this situation? I've dealt with a lot in my life, but someone close to me getting sick is not one of them.

How do you stand by while another person's life slowly seeps from them?

"Come on, let's get to bed. It's late. We can all talk tomorrow, okay?" She steps back from hugging me. "I made up your room, Amelie. Gannon, you can stay in there or sleep on the couch."

When Aunt Cher moved in, she turned the third bedroom of the house into a gym/office, so there was no third bed.

"We'll figure it out." Amelie talks as if she's on autopilot. "Come on, I'll help you get upstairs."

They disappear to the second floor, and I'm left wondering if Amelie will want me close or relegate me to the couch. Before I messed everything up, there would be no question. I'd sleep in her bed as platonically as Taya or Bevan would. But now ...

How are we ever going to navigate this?

14

I should have come home more often during the school years.

That's the thought that keeps running through my head as I walk through my childhood home. As if being here on a random weekend rather than being at college could have prevented my aunt from getting cancer.

Stage three ovarian cancer. How the hell does a woman who bikes almost eighty miles a week, barely has cheat meals, and got off birth control at twenty-two because she told me the hormones affected her get diagnosed with ovarian cancer? It seems like a cruel joke the universe just doled out.

Three weeks ago, she went to her doctor complaining of abdominal pain, and they sent her for more testing. For three weeks, she's waited around by herself to hear the awful results. Aunt Cher only called me when she knew they'd schedules her for chemotherapy because she'd need help.

That was all I'd gotten from her before she demanded I go get some rest. As I helped her into the bed and kissed her forehead, it was as if I could literally hear time ticking away. I hate this so much, and we were barely a day in.

"She's asleep." I let Gannon know as I walk into my room.

He's sitting on my violet comforter, a sight I've seen a million times. Though now, it makes my heart crack wide open. My mind flashes back to his body on mine at my desk at school, and I have to shut it down.

"Good. She looks like she needs some rest. What can I get you? Are you hungry? Want a glass of wine?" Gannon is like a puppy, trying to please me until I pat his head.

I know I'm being cold, and it is so out of my nature that it grates on my skin. But I can't seem to snap out of this. I know he's trying to help, trying to be the best friend I've always had, but it feels stilted and try-hard.

"I'm just tired." My gaze lands on my bed.

Immediately, he jumps up, those big hands running smoothly through his dark whiskey-colored hair.

"I'll go sleep on the couch." Gannon turns to walk out of my room after setting my duffel down.

"Wait," I blurt the word out, but then don't know how to follow it up.

How do I tell him that the only thing I want at the end of this hellish day is to lie in bed and have him hold me? And not only because I don't want to be alone, but because *he's* the only person I want comforting me? I've dreamed of lying in bed with him for years, of him holding me as I fall asleep.

Though after we slept together, there is no way of platonically doing this. I've ruined it; we've ruined it. If that never happened, he could be here more fully for me in this time. I know I told him that we're forgetting it, that I don't have space in my brain to think about what's going on between us. But that's bullshit. Because, of course, when faced with whether or not to sleep in the same bed, that's going to be a factor.

"You could stay. Maybe talk to me for a while?" I shuffle my feet like a nervous child.

"Yeah?" Gannon gives me hopeful eyes, and shit, I hate how that innocent yet sexy gaze makes my stomach flip.

"I just can't stand the silence." I shrug as if that's the only reason I'm letting him stay.

"I've never heard your house this quiet." Gannon flops back down onto my bed, and I sit far enough away so that we're not touching.

"Aunt Cher always had the TV on or music playing. Remember that summer she was obsessed with—"

"Justin Bieber." He chuckles. "I remember. Couldn't enter this house without 'Never Say Never' getting stuck in my head. Hey, I can't believe you still have this."

That big body swaggers across my room. I could pick Gannon's walk out of a lineup. A little slow in its gait, like he's putting on a show and wants everyone to watch. Even when it's just us two, I can't pull my eyes from him.

Gannon plucks a woodshop project from the shelf. It's a heart, though the one side is lumpy and misshapen where he couldn't get the angle on the saw right. There is a chunk missing from the left side, probably from someone dropping it over the years. There is splotchy red spray paint that almost looks orange it's so faded now. But I would never throw it out.

Gannon made that heart for me. In seventh grade, one of the first projects in our woodshop class was to make a paperweight for our parents. To show them we loved them. Well, he didn't want to give one to his mother, so he made it for me.

That heart has sat proudly on the floating shelves in my bedroom for years. I'd look at it most nights in high school and wonder whether or not he knew my heart belonged to him.

"You made it for me." I shrug, those words taking on a whole new meaning after what's gone down between us.

A smoldering gaze finds me, and I would give anything to know what's going on in his brain. On the other hand, I would give anything to stop him from telling me. My mind is over-loaded, and I can't handle this right now. Why is this happening when I don't have room for it? After years of me pining, *now* is the time our relationship decides to take a turn?

"Can we lie down?" I ask, my eyes suddenly feeling so droopy.

Per usual, I'm weak. And that's doubled in this scenario. The only thing I want to console me from reality is him, even though he's part of that harsh reality.

Gannon walks across the room, and my heart beats in time with his steps.

"Come here." He opens his arms, reaching for me, and I let him almost carry me further onto the bed and situate us so that we're lying together.

Tears spring to my eyes, that's how good being held by him is. He's home, my comfort, the one person I can lean on. But he's also the man I'm head over heels in love with. My heart picks up speed as I feel him pull me in. The way my head fits perfectly into the crook of his shoulder and neck. How his legs tangle with mine. How the weight of him is like a security blanket, suppressing all of my anxiety.

"Just close your eyes. I've got you." His voice brushes the lobe of my ear, and I sigh.

It's the best I've felt in forty-eight hours, and I can't deny that this relief comes at the hands of the guy I've always been in love with.

Aunt Cher comes downstairs as I'm cracking eggs into a pan.

"Do you want tomatoes and spinach in your omelet?" I ask, knowing her order.

"That would be great, honey, thank you." She smiles.

At least she doesn't look as tired this morning as she did when Gannon and I arrived last night.

"Did you sleep okay?" she asks, and I turn to find her smiling at me.

But I know that smile. I narrow my eyes as I find a whisk and beat the eggs and milk together. "What?"

Aunt Cher shrugs, picking up the mug of tea I've already set down for her. "I just noticed that the couch wasn't made up. Gannon still asleep?"

Leave it to my aunt to be fighting cancer and still trying to get me laid. By Gannon, of course. She's been meddling with us since we were preteens.

I roll my eyes at her. "Yes, he's still asleep."

"So that's in your bed, I'd assume. Man, things sure have changed from this summer when you wouldn't even go near him at the grocery store."

So my aunt may or may not have seen me hide behind a display of floor cleaner to avoid Gannon and his younger brothers seeing me at Wegman's. It's true that I refused to talk to him this summer. Cher knows how mad I was at him for the whole reality show. She watched it weekly and would text me that the whole thing was a crock of shit and not to get my panties tangled. But I couldn't help it.

"We're friends. And he's slept in my bed before."

"Hmm. But not after a fight like the one you had. And come on, sweets, I know how you feel about him. There is something different, I can feel it."

Normally, I tell Aunt Cher everything. She's the first person I called after I lost my virginity on our senior class trip to Disney. She was the one who taught me about tampons and shaving my armpits. I owe it to her that I know how to apply mascara in a moving car.

For some reason, though, I can't broach this subject, whether it be my confusion about Gannon or her diagnosis. Maybe it's because I'm actively lying to myself that nothing is happening. Maybe I need nothing to happen to keep my full focus on getting her healthy.

Gannon enters the room and the conversation ceases.

"Morning." His rough morning grumble does dangerous things to my insides.

Damn, couldn't I have just stayed in that numb state I'd been in when Cher had first told me the news? It was so much easier to block everything else out, like the fact that I had mind-blowing sex with Gannon.

Now, I am desperately trying not to ogle him in those gray sweatpants he insists on wearing.

"Good morning, sleepy head." Aunt Cher gives him her best grin, though it's only at about half-wattage.

I have to ignore the mental picture of Gannon's big body taking up more than half of the bed this morning. I admit, I stared for an extra few seconds. His back muscles rippled with a yawn as he turned over to hug my pillow when I tried to silently creep out of the room. It was a sight I'd dreamed a million times, and yet I had to leave him for something more important.

A pang echoes through my heart. Cher is this weak and sick, and treatment hasn't even begun. I'm going to get to the bottom of what exactly that involves. I'd say right now was the perfect time.

"So, when is your first appointment?" I dive in as soon as we all sit down.

I've whipped up a breakfast of champions in my nervous state. Her favorite omelets for all three of us, turkey bacon I found in the freezer, fresh pressed orange juice, and a bowl full to the brim with fresh fruit. I'm the cook out of all my friends, and being in the kitchen never fails to settle my anxiety.

It's not weird that Gannon is here for this, and neither of us bat an eye or ask him to leave the room. He's been as much a part of this little family as anyone.

She sets down her green tea and swallows the sip. "Chemo starts tomorrow, so someone will have to drive me. You could stay or pick me up after."

"Of course, I'm staying." I roll my eyes as if she's insane to even suggest that.

"I have chemo once a week, every three weeks for six cycles. Then they'll run a bunch of tests to see if the tumor shrunk, or if I need surgery. They may have to do a full hysterectomy."

The way she winces when she says that last word, I want to break down into sobs. I know what it means, though I always equate that surgery to an older woman. But Aunt Cher is still young. Still able to have children naturally if she met someone and wanted to. This disease, that surgery, would take away that ability. My entire body feels like a ton of bricks was just dropped onto it.

"Aunt Cher ..." I whisper, everything on the table suddenly looking unappetizing.

"Nope, we're not doing that." It's Gannon who speaks up, then points to Aunt Cher. "Do you know who this woman is? She once lifted an entire tree branch off my leg and carried me to the car, and I must have been double her weight at the time. This is one of the strongest women I know, and she's going to fight like a warrior."

"Damn right I am, handsome." Aunt Cher winks at him, but I can tell she has a lump of emotion behind her words.

I blink the tears back, swallowing rapidly. "Yes, you are. Okay, so we have a few weeks of on and off? I'll have to ask your doctors for a supply list, what to buy for home, join some ovarian cancer Facebook groups ..."

Nodding at Gannon across the table, he reaches for my hand and finds it on my thigh. My entire flesh goose bumps.

"I'm sorry, Amelie." Aunt Cher is the one who is breaking now, her eyes the same blue that my mom had, turning glassy.

"For what?" I'm confused.

She blows out an emotional breath. "You've already been through so much in your life. If I could have hidden this, if there were anyone else around to help ... you wouldn't have to be here. You shouldn't have to do this. It's so unfair. I hate that I'm pulling you away from school, I hate that you're—"

"Stop it," I bite out, physically appalled that she could think any of this. "You're not pulling me from anything. You're not a burden, I don't wish I wasn't here. You're the person I love most in my life, and there is nothing more important than being here for you. It's not your fault you got sick, and the only thing we can do now is fight. I don't want to hear that again."

I shove my chair back and walk around the table to squeeze her into a hug. The sigh she releases into my shoulder tells me she's been holding this guilt since she found out about her diagnosis.

"Well, good to know you love her more than me." Gannon harrumphs in a joking manner, breaking the tension.

Both Aunt Cher and I crack up laughing and back away, wiping our eyes. This is why I brought him along. Gannon always knows the right thing to say at the best moment, and he knows us better than anyone. He knows when he can joke with us and when we just need a shoulder to cry on.

But ... if only he knew just how much I do love him.

15

Both nights that I sleep with Amelie pulled tight against me, I have to wake up and go directly to the bathroom. Simply so that I can jack off before my best friend, who is in a delicate mental state, doesn't discover that I'm hard and thick as a sledgehammer. It's fucking torture, my cock wedged in between the most perfect ass I've ever seen, and I can't do a damn thing.

I should not be thinking about undressing her with my teeth and hearing those heavenly noises she makes. Not at a time like this. But I can't fucking help it. For the first time in the history of our relationship, I have an excuse to hold her in my arms as she falls asleep. I'm comforting her, right? That's at least what we can convince ourselves of while all of these feelings brew under the surface.

Not that being home in Webton has been that bad. I returned for a few weeks in the summer after filming wrapped, just to check in and take care of my brothers and sisters. I like my adopted hometown, it's a quaint place with families who genuinely love each other. It's got that white picket feel I always sought but now reject in favor of fame.

Two days ago, I met Quinn at our favorite burger joint, Ollie's, to go over my current sponsorship and brand deals. She also got word about a TV pilot that might be interested in testing me out for a role. That got my blood pumping. I know I swore I'd stay at Talcott until graduation, but the longer I sit in classes, the more bored I get. Before I got cast on the show, my marketing major seemed like a good gig to follow. I'd be good at it, make decent money, be able to live more comfortably and securely than I ever had before.

But now I'd been bitten, as they say, and I want to chase the high of stardom and acting. How cliché am I?

Cher and Amelie just got home from Cherry's chemo treatment, and I've decided to surprise them with heaping cups of frozen yogurt.

"Extra gummy worms? You know the way to my heart." Cher's voice is gravelly and meek, but she smiles as she takes her bright green plastic spoon from me.

This week has been hell for her. I can't imagine six more of them, but if it means she lives and kicks this cancer's ass, then it's what will have to happen.

"Thanks for this." Amelie thanks me with a contented sigh as she scoops into her chocolate-flavored yogurt with cheesecake bites.

"Honestly? I just wanted some of my own," I admit.

We settle into the gray sectional in Cher's living room; I'm in the middle with the two women cuddled up at either end with their elbows sinking into the arms. As naturally as ever, Amelie leans over far enough to stick her spoon in my red velvet flavored cup and take a big taste.

"Mooch." I grin at her.

"Hey, it's not my fault that we have traditions." She shrugs.

I knew she'd do it. Just like I knew that she'd ask to steal one of the sour peach rings I put in my cup as well. And right after we finish these, I know she'll lie down and ask for her favorite white fuzzy blanket from the back of the couch. Which I'll throw over her and then rest my hand on her feet, which she'll eventually wiggle to get me to rub them.

I know her like the back of my hand. More than ever, now that I know what kind of face she makes when she comes. God, this is torture.

I'm stuck between a rock and a hard place, and no matter what I do, I'm hurting someone.

I'd finally come to the decision, after I was inside Amelie and couldn't hide my feelings any longer, that I'd come out and tell her. On that awful drive to the pharmacy to correct a mistake I'd made out of stupidity, I was about to spill everything. Tell her that I've always been in love with her, that she is the only woman who occupies my thoughts and heart. I wanted to ask her to be with me, to give us a real shot. My past, my history, the mother who set the examples be damned. I knew, after we were together, that there was no turning back.

And then she'd gotten that phone call. So I couldn't tell her. Then she'd made it explicitly clear that we were forgetting what happened, not talking about it, and she had bigger things to focus on.

I've thought about the words I would have said to her had that phone not rung. I think about them every single day. It's killing me inside not to confess that I love her. That I've been an idiot for too many years, trying to shut those feelings down. But it would hurt her just as bad if I made this about me or us right now, while she's fighting to keep her aunt alive. She doesn't need that shit on her mind. She doesn't need to accept these feelings from me, or reject them, God forbid, when she's worried about the only family she has left.

So I stay silent. It's a form of agony I wouldn't wish on anyone. Being able to sleep beside her, rub her feet, be here for her every need, but then not able to voice what's going on in my heart.

"We have to talk about a plan for you about school, Amelie." Aunt Cher grabs her own blanket, and I move hastily to help tuck her into it.

She smiles appreciatively and hands me her half-full yogurt cup. The chemo seems to have taken her appetite. She looks so frail, like if I touch her, she might break.

"What is there to talk about?" Ams is avoiding the conversation, just like she has for the last three days.

Any time Cher or I bring up Talcott, Ams shuts down. I don't know who this person is. I know she's going through hell, but Amelie is quite literally the most positive, most caring person I know. She doesn't have a mean bone in her body, and yet I've seen her snap on several occasions since we got to Webton.

She's been talking to me, at most times, like she'd rather punch me instead of talk. The only time she softens and lets me see the her I know and love is when we're falling asleep together in her bed.

"Amelie, you can't just quit college. You have to go back at some point. I can hire a service, I have the money to do that. There are single people who get themselves to and from chemo all the time."

Cher doesn't sound so certain of that, but I don't say anything. Do I want her here alone? Hell fucking no. But do I want Amelie to throw away her life and dreams to watch another member of her family die? That's an even bigger hell no.

Amelie snorts out a sardonic pfft. "That's bullshit, and you know it. No way am I leaving you here to get to freaking chemotherapy by yourself."

It does sound pretty dumb, but I stay out of it still.

"And no way am I letting you drop out of college." Cher puts on her best no-nonsense mothering tone.

"Don't go all 'young lady' on me." Ams rolls her eyes.

The two glare at each other, annoyed by the other's love and need to watch over them.

"You have a full life to live, Amelie. You have friends and a job and classes. How am I ever going to live my dreams of being married in the New York Public Library like Carrie Bradshaw if I don't have a connection to do so? I'm counting on you."

Cherry is referring to the *Sex and the City* movie, which they've made me watch a dozen or more times.

"Technically, Carrie never got married there. Actually, it ended in disaster." Amelie raises one eyebrow.

"See? I'll do what Carrie never could. Who could top a wedding like that? I need you for that." Cher sticks her tongue out at her.

"I don't want to leave you." Amelie's voice goes quiet.

"You're not." Her aunt's eyes soften. "You came right home to help. And I love you for it. But I need you to chase your dreams, so I have a couch to crash on in the Big Apple when I get better. We'll figure out a plan, but promise me you won't leave college?"

There is a long pause, but Amelie finally nods like it's a fight she was never going to win.

I want to gather her up in my arms and promise her, just like she promised Cherry, that everything will work out.

But I don't know that, in terms of any of the issues at play here.

We stay with Aunt Cher for a week, with me driving back and forth to Talcott.

I've already missed so much school, I literally cannot afford to miss in-person classes or I'll likely be asked to leave the college. Amelie is, of course, granted a week of leave due to family circumstances, but because I'm not blood-related, I can't claim the same.

It's fine. I don't mind driving back and forth just to be there for them. But as the first week of chemo came to a close, Cher was itching for Ams to get back to school. So, like they said they would, they made a compromise.

Cherry insisted on Amelie returning to Talcott for the weeks between her chemotherapy treatments. During the off weeks, she and Amelie agreed that a hired nursing care service would care for her. I know Amelie isn't happy with this deal, but we all know she can't just quit college.

We've been back at school for two days, and Ams has been quiet. The first night we were home, I cooked her dinner, and we sat on the back deck of the house drinking beer with the rest of our roommates.

Today is the first time we've been separated for any real period because we both had classes and she's been at her job in the library for about four hours.

I'm waiting on the couch watching a playoff baseball game when she comes in. Rising to meet her, I feel my nervous energy dissipate. I guess I didn't realize it until now, but I've been on edge being away from her for so long. And when the hell did that start happening? It's like I've given a name to the feelings I've always had for her, and suddenly I'm a junkie, unable to let my drug out of my sight.

"How was your shift?" I ask her as she pulls her school bag over her head.

I take it from her and hang it on one of the hooks in the foyer. Then I reach behind her to lock the door. It helps me feel better when I'm helping her, even if it's the smallest of things.

"Long, but good. Nothing like being in a library and organizing carts full of new books to get my mind off of things." She smiles, and it's small, but at least it's the first real one I think I've seen in a week.

"You and your books. I used to lose you in the Webton Library, remember that?" The memory makes me chuckle.

"That's because you refused to learn where the sections were. How many times did I drag you in and you couldn't memorize where teen fiction was?"

I shrug. "Books were never my thing."

But I went, almost every day after school from sixth to tenth grade, because Amelie loved it. I'd hang out while she browsed, either on my phone or at one of the computer terminals. Sometimes, I'd simply watch her decision-making process as she'd come back with an armful of books.

"That's probably why you're glued to TikTok. Never learned to read so you just watch video."

My hand flies to my chest, and I pretend to be shocked. "Was that a joke? Coming from Amelie Brook? God, haven't heard one of those in weeks!"

She walks into the living room while looking over her shoulder and rolling her eyes at me. "I've had a lot of things on my plate, if you didn't notice."

Now she's biting her lip, and I want to facepalm myself. I just made her think of Aunt Cher rather than distracting her with jokes. My course of conversation backfired.

"Want to watch something?" I try again. "There is a *Parks & Rec* marathon on Comedy Central."

Amelie shrugs. "Sure."

But she's on her phone, and that's so unlike her. I know she's probably trying to check in with Cher for updates or is trying to log into the health portal to see doctor's notes. Cher gave her access on Amelie's insistence, another compromise, since she can't be there the whole time.

The girl loses her phone in her backpack more than she's on it, the only Gen Z-er I've ever met who isn't obsessed with social media. So I know something is deeply wrong.

"Or we could talk about it." I'm not pulling my punches.

Amelie looks up and blinks those big hazel eyes at me.

She sniffles, and I immediately reach for her. Pulling her tight against me on the couch, my arms wrap around protectively as she begins to cling to my shirt.

I hold her, expecting the sobs to come, but they don't. Amelie just seems to sigh into me, as if she needed a port in the storm and this is a relief rather than a place to breakdown. My heart dissolves, beating so fast that I can't seem to take a full breath. Both because I can offer her this comfort, and because it's felt like an eternity since I've been allowed to freely touch her.

Memories of that night in her room assault me, and I have to put tension in my arms to keep them from shaking with need. My hands want to roam, but this is about her. Not me.

Plus, Amelie made it crystal clear; she's not interested in anything like that. We made a mistake, were those her words or the ones I interpreted from her statement? She needs me as a friend, not a guy who fucked up and came inside her without a condom. Damn, what did I expect? I hadn't treated her or our time together with any forethought or respect. Of course, she wasn't into giving me a second chance.

I pull back a fraction, but it backfires on me. I mean to tell her that everything is going to be okay. I mean to comfort her and be the best friend she needs.

Instead, our noses brush, and a small whoosh of air releases from Amelie's lungs.

It's not me who pushes the envelope this time. It's her. Amelie doesn't even take a pause before pressing right through whatever agreement we had, whatever boundary she put between us, and kisses me.

The meeting of our mouths might be slow and gentle, a less frenzied exploration than the drunken hookup we had, but it doesn't make it any less passionate. These movements feel like sweet, slow-churned butter: smooth and hot and melting all over. There is an unbridled desire in controlled movements, so molten and scalding that I feel like my body could combust.

There is something to be said about going slow, about the tension that you just know will brim over into uncontrollable pleasure. Sex has always been a release, but with Amelie, it's so much more. There is meaning behind this, importance, mutual love. I've never experienced that in physical affection, and it makes my head spin.

I flip us, one hand splayed on her back as the other bypasses the hem of her shirt to reach under and tickle at the warm skin of her waist. Amelie's palms are on my cheeks, maneuvering my face so that our tongues can push deeper into each other's mouths.

We're making out on the couch like two teenagers, and I have no intention of stopping this. I know what Amelie said, but I'm a greedy man. If she initiated this, I'm going to seal the deal. I'm going to show her, this time, how much I care about her. And after we're done, I'm not letting her leave my bed for a week.

"Gross, Gannon. At least take your skanks upstairs before you hump them. I do not need to see this on a weekday."

Bevan's condescending voice cuts through the haze of passion that was forming like a rose-colored cloud around us.

I'm both flying and being pushed off of Amelie in seconds. She scrambles up, fixing her hair and fidgeting wildly.

"Am!" Bevan's jaw practically unhinges she's so floored. "I ... holy shit, I couldn't see you ... holy shit!"

The three of us stand there in awkward shock before Bevan's attitude flips from surprise to anger.

"Upstairs, now!" She points her finger to the second floor, ordering Amelie around like a child.

"Ams, let's go to my room." I hedge my bets, knowing that between the two of us, she's probably not going to pick me.

I don't even want her to come to the attic to continue what we were doing. Well, I wouldn't be opposed to it. But really, I just want to talk about all of the stuff we need to lay down on the table.

Her pretty blond head swivels back and forth before landing on Bevan.

"I'll meet you up there in a couple minutes, okay?"

Obviously, I was never going to be the dog she picked. It still stings like hell, though, when she chooses her girlfriend over me. And now I feel like I've dug myself even further into this hole. My best friend almost shut me out after I kissed her the first time. What's going to happen now?

I don't know what to do at this point; I feel helpless. Amelie doesn't want to discuss what happened between us, but she kissed me. I don't want to shackle her to me if I admit we both love each other, but I can't stay away. My carefully laid defenses, the ones I've built up since I knew she was way too good for me all the way back when we were ten, have crumbled, and I don't know where to hide.

Plus, I don't even want to hide. Now I'm the one who wants to turn our friendship into more, and she's the one who is avoiding it.

My, how the tables have turned.

"You're sleeping with Gannon? You're *sleeping* with Gannon!"

Taya has been repeating this over and over for the last three minutes.

The three of us are sitting on her bed, our usual spot for downloading the latest news in our lives and venting about petty gossip. It feels good to be in their presence, and I realize I've barely seen them the last two weeks. Come to think of it, I've barely told them anything that's been going on. Taya and Bevan have been supportive, but I think they're a little freaked out that I'll lash out and revert back to how I was after my parents passed.

"I'm not sleeping with him." I sigh in exhaustion, because I already know this conversation will take it out of me. "Well, once. We slept together once."

"WHAT?" Bevan looks like a tea kettle that just blew its top. "You finally had sex with Gannon Raferty and didn't tell us *immediately*? If that were me, my panties wouldn't have even been dry from his—"

"Okay!" I hold up a hand. "I didn't tell you because things

were chaotic and then the next morning I found out about Aunt Cher. And so, that took precedence. I've barely had time to process it in the first place, let alone tell you."

"But you had time to make out and dry hump him on the couch?" Bevan raises an inquisitive eyebrow at me.

"I thought something happened that night, but I couldn't be sure ... never expected *this*, though." Taya looks truly stunned.

"Wait, I thought Jameson was here the other night." Bevan looks confused. "Which night was it? I feel like my world is upside down."

"That party the night before I found out about Cher. And yes, Jameson was here." That makes me feel more miserable.

"Does he know?" Taya asks, not out of judgment, but because it would be one more thing for me to deal with.

I hate hurting people, and she knows that if I told him or when I do, I'll feel really bad about it.

"No. Not yet. Just another stop on the tour of hell I'm apparently on." Which I've been putting off, or maybe just forgot about.

"Any other secrets you need to divulge?" Bevan's eyes are wide.

"Well, that and I had to get the morning after pill." I say it nonchalantly and then realize my mistake when I look at their faces.

"You took Plan B and didn't tell us?" Now it's Taya's turn to go apeshit.

"I kind of had a lot of things going on that day," I grumble, rolling my eyes at her.

"We know." Bevan squeezes my hand in a rare moment of sensitivity. "How do you feel after taking it? Was it bad?"

Neither of them has ever taken it, I know this for a fact. They would have told me. Sheesh, I probably would have been the one to drive them to CVS. But I've been so wrapped up in every-

Just About Over You

thing else that I've barely had time to process that I took the morning after pill. It's a big deal, aside from everything else. If it was the only thing going on in my life, I probably would have laid in bed and contemplated that decision for a few hours. I wouldn't have done it differently, but for me, it was a moment.

"I felt okay. Honestly, I was so focused on Cher that it was probably a good thing I wasn't too focused on it. Had some cramping and bleeding like I would during a period. Other than that, nothing too crazy. I just can't believe I didn't stop him so he could put on a condom. I was so caught up."

"Sometimes, the best sex happens that way." Bevan looks wistful.

"So does unplanned pregnancy." Taya glares at her. "I'm glad you got the pill, though. And ... is it Team Gannon of me if I say I'm glad you finally did the deed? Just to at least see what it was like."

"What was it like?" Now Bevan wiggles her eyebrows at me.

My cheeks turn a shade of light pink. I'm all for discussing and being open with my best girlfriends, but there is something different about telling them about sex with Gannon.

"Incredible. Hot. Fast. Like we were trying to unload years of pent-up tension." I squeeze my thighs together just thinking about it.

"Gah, you have that thoroughly satisfied face, and I'm jealous. I miss sex." Taya pouts over her long-distance relationship.

"Preaching to the choir." Bevan sighs miserably.

We all know how loud and eventful her and Callum's sex life was.

"Why is this happening now?" I whine, flopping face down into the bed.

I feel Taya begin to rub my back. "Maybe because it's the perfect time, even if you can't see it."

"But we've resolved nothing. I can still barely address what happened on the show, or the sex, and there is just too much. Now with Cher, I just feel so emotionally drained. I've wanted him for so long, you guys know that. But it just feels like something I can't handle right now. I wanted this to be butterflies and rainbows, and instead it's happening at the worst possible time. Hell, I don't even know if it's real. Maybe he's just horny and woke up one day thinking I looked decent."

Bevan's eyes are fiery as I turn over to face my friends. "I would hope that's not what he's doing, because it would jeopardize a really great friendship in the name of getting off. Which is so like a man to do, but I'm not sure that's what is happening here."

"I don't think so at all." Taya rushes to jump in, considering Bev might not be the best advice giver on love these days. "Can we please not assume love comes with balloons and romantic gestures? You do remember how Austin and I got together, right?"

Since high school, Taya had a crush on Austin, but it wasn't until he sublet Gannon's empty room last semester that they even had a shot at something. Then he found this love letter she wrote him when she was fifteen, and she was so embarrassed they almost didn't happen. When she puts it that way, I guess that love isn't all candlelit dinners and walks in the moonlight.

"I can't, though. Not right now. What if something worse happens to Aunt Cher? What if Gannon decides this isn't worth it when I've already let all of my walls down? I was right there, guys, so close to finally giving someone else another chance. It was like he knew that."

"*Men*." Bevan rolls her eyes. "They come groveling the moment they know you're not thinking about them anymore."

"Ain't that the truth." Taya snorts. "I want you to be happy, Am. And I don't want you to be worrying about what he's thinking if you already have so much on your plate. But at the same time ..."

She trails off and looks to Bevan. "Hey, don't look at me. I said fuck men and am miserable. I think it's been years of this bullshit with Gannon and if I don't say that, I'd be lying."

And above all, we don't lie to each other.

"I know. I don't know what to do. I told him it's a nonstarter. But I mean, I still let him kiss me. Because, my lord, that guy can kiss."

Taya and Bevan start in again, and of course, the next question is how big is his dick? We've all almost seen it this one time when Gannon flashed a bunch of people at a high school bonfire. But now that I know the dirty details ...

The girl talk helps, but I'm still all sorts of confused. There is too much going on right now to give this a chance. But at the same time, when I'm around him, he's always the only thing I can focus on.

Moving forward, I think my best option is to just keep my distance. There is still so much that needs to be discussed; about the years I've loved him, about his time on the show, how that hurt me terribly. And I don't have the energy to do it all right now. So those things would have to be discussed before I could even consider letting myself be open to something with Gannon.

For the first time since my secret love for him started, I'm coming at it from a rational place instead of mooning over him like all my fairy tales are about to come true.

Classes are a blur in the weeks I'm back at Talcott.

It feels like I'm just waiting for the weeks to end so I can race back to Webton and care for Aunt Cher. This life I'm leading is a double one, and it feels odd that acquaintances on campus don't know what I'm going through. What started out as a great year, despite my feud with Gannon, has now turned into this purgatory.

I don't feel like I fit at Talcott, but I feel like something is calling me back when I'm in my hometown.

Library jobs are hard to come by, and the one I want to go for is even more competitive. But I've barely had time to look at the application for the New York Library internship, and I almost don't even care at this point. I don't feel like myself. The things I held dear don't mean a lick now that Aunt Cher's health is in question.

She says she's feeling okay, but the nurses update me. I know she's vomiting a lot, has little energy or appetite. The chemo is taking it out of her, and I'm worried day and night.

Those feelings I had after my parents' death threaten to fall over me like an immovable veil. I was a zombie that year, trudging through life as if I was numb. I can't let that feeling take over this time, because I have someone to fight for. It's really tough, though, not to give in.

That dark place is creeping in on me as I walk through campus, barely acknowledging my surroundings.

"Amelie!"

I turn to the voice calling my name and find Jameson almost smack dab in front of me.

"Oh, Jameson!" I squeak, thoroughly surprised.

He looks like he usually does; a happy, upbeat guy with pretty brown hair and eyes. He's tall, but of course, everyone is to me, and Jameson just has that nice guy aura that makes everyone want to talk to him.

Well, except for me right now.

If I'm being honest, I completely forgot about him. It's been two and a half weeks since I first went home to help Aunt Cher with chemo, and I've neither texted him myself nor heard from him on his own accord in that time.

We had a date planned for two days after I slept with Gannon at that party. I was going to tell him then that I'd technically but not technically cheated on him. Then life got in the way, and I had to cancel. To do so, I had to tell him what was going on, but in the most sparing of details. Jameson answered with concern and well wishes but hadn't reached out since.

Honestly, now that I think about it, a guy who was really into me would have at least checked in a few times. But who am I to judge? I feel immense guilt that I slept with someone else while we were in the early stages of seeing each other.

"How have you been?" He moves in to give me a hug, and I go stiff.

This feels off, having someone comfort me who doesn't know Aunt Cher ... and honestly doesn't know me. I'm a very positive, caring person, but I also keep my circle small. I cherish the few people I love, because giving them all of the love in me is one of my biggest priorities. I don't want quantity over quality.

"Um ... decent," I answer, because I don't really know how.

I mean, I haven't been decent. Okay seems too strong of a word for what I've been. I can't say horrible because that's not something you say to a boy you've slept with but who also doesn't know you on a deeper level.

"I can't imagine, I'm so sorry. Is your aunt feeling okay?"

Jameson means well, but his oblivious questions just hurt.

"She's not, really. But, um, could we sit?" I ask, my heart beating wildly.

Guilt coats the walls of my stomach and throat like slime, and I have no idea how I'm going to push these words out. Hurting people is my worst fear, and I'm about to hurt someone in the worst way.

"Absolutely." He jumps to it, finding us an open bench and ushering me over.

He thinks I'm about to unload on him, have him be my shoulder. But if he really wanted that, shouldn't he have come to see me sooner?

None of this is his fault, but perhaps I shouldn't feel so bad about what happened with Gannon. Maybe it wasn't as serious as I thought Jameson might think it was.

"Tell me, how have you really been?" Sincerity is painted on his face.

Ugh, I thought right. He thinks I need a hand to hold.

"Yeah, um, that's not really what I need to talk to you about. I need to talk about us." I motion, trying to use hand gestures to explain.

"Oh, sure." Something flickers over Jameson's face, but I can't place it.

I forge on, even though everything in me wants to run away.

"I slept with someone else. The night of the party you were

at, before I found out about my aunt." I just blurt it out, not knowing any other way to relay the information.

"What the fuck?" Jameson rears back like I've smacked him. "I was there that night."

I rub the back of my hand violently, as if I'm trying to remove the invisible spots of shame dotting my body like a rash. "I know you were. I'm so sorry, Jameson. It just happened, one thing led to another and—"

"Please, I don't need details of how you fucked another guy, Amelie." He holds up a hand.

Now it's my turn to feel slapped. That was harsh, but I can't blame the guy.

"I'm sorry, Jameson. I really am. It was a situation I felt was out of my control—"

"Wait, you're saying this guy attacked you?" Now his anger turns to worry.

I throw up my hands like stop signs. "No, not at all. Sorry I just meant ... the feelings I had for this guy were a long time coming and—"

"Oh, shit. Shit. You slept with your roommate, didn't you? Gannon, right? I always knew that guy was trash ..."

"Hey." My voice is a low note of warning. "Nothing that happened between him and I had anything to do with you, and you don't know him."

You barely know me, I want to say.

"So, you're sitting here, trying to apologize to me for screwing someone else while we were going out, and now you're defending him? *Classy*."

The haughty nature of his words makes me want to crawl under the bench, but they also show colors that I didn't know he was capable of.

My eyes narrow. "I am apologizing, Jameson. What I did was wrong, and I'm sorry for that."

I'm not going to sit here and make excuses, or explain how this is so much bigger than just a hookup with Gannon. I could delve into the fact that we didn't have a title and weren't really committed, but that's a cop-out. I'll sit in the shame, even if he's going to get ugly.

Jameson stands, glowering down at me. "Whatever. I was talking to girls on the side anyway."

And then he stomps off. His parting words were meant as a bullet, but they're only a slight pinch. Part of me isn't surprised since he looked panicked when I said I needed to talk about us. Another part of me kind of knew it, because college guys were always talking to multiple girls, right?

Still, this doesn't feel good. It stings to do this to someone, even if I didn't see a future after all the other events that have happened in the past few weeks.

Again, it's just another person retreating from my life. Some days, when I'm at my lowest, I believe it's because of me.

I don't have another option.

As I stare at my broken tripod and the body scrub on the bed next to it, I bite my lip. Fuck, I'm going to have to ask one of my roommates for help with this, and that's going to be embarrassing as shit.

Now, you might think that whatever I'm about to do is some kinky shit. Maybe to some it is. But to me, it's a paycheck. Specifically, one for a coffee body scrub that is supposed to invigorate your skin in the shower. So, the company wants me shirtless, rubbing this shit all over my abs for an Instagram video. Which is fine, I've done worse for money. But my tripod broke this morning, so I can't shoot it myself and leave my roommates none the wiser about the activities that go on in the attic.

Reluctantly, I creep out of my top floor hideaway in search of someone. Hopefully, Scott is around because even though he'll mock me relentlessly, at least I won't have to ask one of the girls. Bevan would hurl some insult at me or try to stab me *Psycho* style while I was in the shower. No way would Taya help, she'd laugh in my face as if this was the dumbest job ever.

And good lord, there is no way I would want Amelie

anywhere near this. We've been in this weird dance as of late. Both of us act like nothing is wrong when we do happen to bump into each other, even though our voices are at their highest decibels of fake nice and political correctness. Then the rest of the time, we're definitely avoiding each other.

Ever since Bevan walked in on us on our way to fuck again, Amelie has been skittish. Plus, she's about to leave for Webton and Aunt Cher's treatments again, so I won't see her for close to a week. I hate this limbo. I wish I could just tell her how I feel, but that brings us back to the root of the problem of not over-loading her.

Taya told me that Amelie ran into Jameson, and it hadn't gone well. He called her mean, or some shit like it, and that was such a fucking underhanded move that I wanted to punch the guy. Amelie is the nicest person I've ever met. I'm the one who made her screw up, and now he's convinced she's some kind of ...

The thought makes me clench my fists with rage. He has no idea who she is, and damn him for not seeing through any bull-shit to understand that. Although, I guess that's better for me, since he's out of the picture. On one hand, I want everyone in the world to think of her as the sweet, nurturing person she is. On the other, if Jameson's opinion of her keeps him away, I might be okay with that.

When I make it downstairs, the whole house is pretty quiet.

Peering out to the driveway from the front window, I only see two cars out there. Mine. And Amelie's.

Shit, this is just great. I wander into the living room, and there she sits. Her laptop is in her lap, her legs crossed, with earbuds in. She's gently swaying to whatever she's listening to, and she looks like a goddamn angel with a halo.

All of that ethereal blond hair is piled in a spun nest on top of her head. Her face is makeup free, like it usually is, and I can make out the slight beauty mark just above the right side of her upper lip. In leggings and an oversized Webton Football long sleeve that was once mine, she looks more beautiful than any of the Instagram models I've met.

The pearls in her earlobes are so innocent, which only makes them that much hotter to me.

Amelie is sin wrapped in innocence. If she lets you in to see underneath her skin, you'll be privy to the sexy siren underneath. At least that's how I remember it when she was pinned beneath me, moaning as she came on my cock.

Fuck, do I wish that could happen again.

"I need help," I grumble, looking away sullenly.

"Huh?" Amelie pulls an AirPod out.

"I said I need help with something." I look at her, and my stomach dips.

This is going to force me to completely swallow my pride.

"Okay … what is it?" Ams is thoroughly confused.

"I need to shoot an ad campaign for an Instagram partnership I have. But my tripod broke. You're the only one home. Would you, um, help me?"

A beat passes, and I hate that I asked. I should have just rigged the thing to the bathroom counter and propped it up with books. We haven't spoken in days, and the first thing I ask her for is help with a social media campaign? She hates all that, and I should just be a man and come out with it all.

But my reservations are holding me back.

Ams bites her bottom lip, and damn do I want to tackle her back into the couch where we were just days ago. "Yeah, I can help."

It's sad that she sounds reluctant, because before all of this happened between us, she'd be the first person I'd go to. We would have laughed our asses off about me having to scrub coffee grounds into my stomach. Ams would have blushed while I made sexually explicit jokes.

Now, I can just foresee it, this is going to be so incredibly awkward; my spine already aches from the tension.

"The thing is, I ... uh, I have to be shirtless. And in the shower. So, you're going to have to video that."

As predicted, Amelie's beautiful unblemished skin goes scarlet. "You don't have a backup tripod?"

I hadn't thought of that, but it would be a good investment considering this situation.

"No, and I really need to shoot it today for the company. Do you think you could help real quick?"

She nods, more to herself like she's trying to talk her mind into it. "Yeah. Yeah. Right now?"

"If you can?" I shrug awkwardly.

She unfolds from her position on the couch and rises to follow me.

We walk up the stairs quietly. I hate this. Amelie and I are constantly talking when we're around each other. Since I came back from the show, talk has been stilted, angry, or emotional. I miss how it used to be, but understand why it isn't.

When we're in the bathroom, I hand her my phone with the camera app already open and pick up the container of scrub I was sent.

"Woah, well it definitely smells like coffee." Amelie is looking anywhere but at me as I pull my shirt over my head and step into the shower.

The scrub does smell like a Starbucks. "Let's just hope I don't get some sort of rash from this."

"Has it happened before?" she asks as I step into the shower. God, this is awkward.

"This one time, I had to try a charcoal face mask for this one brand. Left me with hives on my cheeks for a week."

"Wait, I remember that." She starts giggling.

"Thanks for the sympathy." I pout. "All right, so just start taking some pictures from all angles, close up, of my whole body, from above, from below."

I'm shouting out directives to her like she's going to know what to do. It doesn't take much skill, but I've been on professional photo shoots before, and I know the jargon. To someone like Amelie, who barely takes pictures because she says she wants to live in the memory, this is so foreign.

"And how much are you making from this?" Amelie looks skeptical as she starts to click pictures.

I'm posing and speak through my smile as I pretend to fake laugh. "Five thousand dollars."

"Five thousand dollars!" She nearly drops the phone.

"Hey, be careful with that," I scold. "And yes. I've been able to get to the place where I can negotiate higher sponsorships. That's honestly on the low end."

"Five grand for a couple of shirtless pictures? Where do I sign up?"

My balls tingle when she says it, but the green monster of jealousy swarms my mind. "You're better than this, than what I do. Plus, I'd probably murder a bunch of dudes trying to look at you topless."

Her intake of breath and the way her cheeks pink up has me wanting to pull her into this coffee scrub with me. I imagine running my gritty hands all over her body; the scrub leaving a trail from her cleavage down to her navel and then lower.

If I don't stop, I'll have a boner. And that will make this interaction even more awkward than it already is.

"I'm close to five hundred thousand followers on Instagram. I'm hoping this ad gets me there." I rub my hands together.

Amelie shakes her head. "I never understand it, this obsession for followers. Why? What do you get out of it?"

Gratification. Attention. The feeling that they love me or at least accept and like me like I never got at home growing up. But I don't say that.

"Each time I hit a certain number, it's like a video game. Unlocking levels of popularity. And those levels lead to money, which leads to what I actually want to do. Hopefully. I'm hoping that at some point I'll land on the radar of a casting director or series creator."

Amelie doesn't look convinced, and I'm sure she's judging me. But the rest of our friends are just as bad. Everyone on this campus is posting pictures and videos to feed the beast of ego, and I'm profiting from mine. Can't blame me for that. In fact, I think it makes me smarter.

"I'd never heard you confess that dream before *Mrs. Right*. You really want to go into acting?"

I try to find the words to make her understand.

"This one time, you told me that reading a book helped you get lost. That for a few moments, you could forget the world and become one of the characters. That always stuck with me. And when I got on that set, even though I was technically playing myself, I was a character. When I did something well, I'd get praise from the producers or directors. And for the few moments I was in a scene, I forgot about all the shit at home. I forgot about my life and the way my mom royally sucks. I wanted to feel the way you do when you get lost in a book. And I think I might have found it."

When I look up, Amelie has dropped her hand to her side, my phone idle, and is just staring at me.

"That ... that makes a lot of sense." She still looks gobsmacked.

It dawns on me that my best friend may or may not have had any faith that I would pick a career I'd stay driven in. A lot of people probably thought that about me. Hell, ask anyone in

Webton about the Raferty kids or mother and they'd turn their noses up.

"So, let's shoot this so I can get one step closer." I wink at Ams.

A couple beats of silent photography while I rub coffee scrub on me, and I feel like we might almost be done.

"Your fans are going to eat this right up. I'm getting some good ones here. I mean, this almost makes *me* want to buy the product." Ams smirks at me, her eyes sparking with mischief.

Is she flirting with me?

"You can use some of mine anytime," I fire right back, my tone laced with innuendo.

"Turn the shower on, pretend to wash some off." She's directing this photo shoot now, getting into it.

I do as I'm told, and the spray hits me. I swear I hear a little gasp, but I don't look at her. If I do that, I might make another move that will only end in more awkwardness.

At some point, though, I can't help it. Our eyes meet over the camera, and heat swamps low in my balls. This feels way more intimate than I intended, and I have to physically bite the inside of my cheek to keep from asking her to come in with me.

We finish up, and I'm confident I can send these to the company and they'll love them.

"I owe you for this. Let's go grab Frappuccinos, all this coffee talk makes me want one," I say as I stand under the spray, washing the scrub off.

"Do your followers know you love a good girly coffee drink? Maybe we should tell them," she jokes, and I can feel her gaze on my body.

We should just talk this out, but it's the friendliest we've been in days.

"Sure, let's get you on my Instagram and we'll go live. You can spill all the tea about me."

Amelie makes an X with her arms. "Absolutely not. I don't want that many people ever knowing what I look like or how my voice sounds."

"Guess they'll never know." I grab a towel from behind the door and dry off.

Amelie now stands just a foot from me, and the bathroom feels claustrophobic. I've slept in beds with this girl, sat in cars for hours-long road trips, had to squish into numerous back seats when there was one too many of us present. But knowing what I know now, and having seen her in her most vulnerable, exposed state, I can't get the thought that I should just kiss her out of my head.

"That's fine. I'll take my Frappuccino as payment and be okay with the fact I'll never get to tell the world that their heart-throb loves whipped coffee drinks."

At least she's agreeing to hang out with me. That I'll take over this weird tension any day.

Even if I have to keep how I feel about her to myself.

Another week in Webton and another week of picking Aunt Cher up off the floor.

Of cleaning up sickness and trying to coax her to eat. Of working with her insurance company and listening to her nurses and doctors.

I'd never say this to her, but I'm miserable. I don't cope well with all of this heavy medical jargon, and hospitals freak me out. It reminds me of the smell on my parents as they laid in their caskets, an image and memory I will never wipe from my mind.

It's morbid, but I always think burying our dead is a creepy thing. The fact that we just have millions of dead bodies in the soil of this country is ... weird. Objectively, extremely weird.

I've told the girls, and Gannon, that I want all of my organs donated and to be cremated. They always tell me it's fucking weird that I give them those instructions, but I don't want them to be forgotten.

I know how fleeting life can be.

Except when Aunt Cher came to me two days ago with a big fat legal envelope in hand. She wanted to discuss her affairs, her accounts, and her wishes.

I shut down. Absolutely not, was I talking about that. And I told her as much.

She called me silly, that of course we had to talk about this because I'd be left confused and panicking if something did happen.

But I can't. I stormed up the stairs of my childhood home and refused to come down for hours, which sucks of me because she was probably uncomfortable or in pain or finally hungry. But there is no reality in which I can plan for the last member of my family's death. Not even hypothetically.

For the first time since her diagnosis, I was happy to come back to Talcott. I couldn't be in that house, the one that used to belong to my parents before they died, thinking about my aunt's last will and testament.

So I was even happier when the public library decided to call me in when they were short-handed.

I'd decided to volunteer in the children's section of the public library near Talcott last year. Working at the one on campus, I only ever saw panicking, procrastinating, or studious co-eds. Here, I could take a break from organizing anthologies and textbooks. Here, I could admire the bright suns the preschool students painted last week that now hung on the wall. Here, I can listen to the trivial questions of little kids and get lost in the fun.

So, once a week I help do story time for the three-year-olds, and it's the highlight of my days right now.

"Miss Amewie?" Sarah, a little girl with a missing front tooth, comes up to me.

I kneel down. "What is it, sweetie?"

"I really like Dr. Seuss. But I don't want to eat green ham." She sticks out her tongue.

I laugh. "Oh no, you don't have to eat green ham. I don't know where we'd even find that! It's just a funny story."

She giggles. "Yeah, it's so silly!"

Then she runs off to play with the other little girls, who are combing through the trains on the table we have in the play corner.

We just finished our circle time featuring the book *Dragons Love Tacos*, which was a real hit with my tiny audience. I grab the stack of books a group of little boys has piled on the floor and walk it back to the reference desk to sort and put away later.

"Thought I'd find you here." Gannon leans against the desk as I turn back around, and my God, he should not be allowed to do that.

In a black T-shirt and jeans, he looks like he belongs on the cover of *GQ*. Chocolate brown waves are perfectly but effortlessly styled above his chiseled face, and his jawline is spotted with the perfect amount of stubble. I swear, they're going to come out with some kind of makeup line that would make men look exactly like this perfect specimen. Or at least they should. They'd probably make a ton of money.

"You do know my schedule and whereabouts most times." I smirk. "Just don't let the kids see you if you want to get out of here quickly."

The reading hour children *love* Gannon with a capital *L*. As if he wasn't already gorgeous and charming enough, but he's the kind of guy that kids are just drawn to, and he's amazing with them. As someone who wants to be a librarian and loves picking books for children, it's pretty hard to ignore that turn-on.

"Quick, hide me in the shelves." He ducks under his hand, pretending to hide.

Gosh, the things I've heard that go on in the shelves of the Talcott Library ...

I've heard, but never witnessed. And thinking about going back there with Gannon? My whole body bursts into goose bumps.

"We can't be caught, because we're on a schedule. I know what you need." Gannon gives me his smirk, the one that has one corner of his mouth turning up while the other lags behind.

It's devastating, that smirk, and so irresistible that I can't even respond.

"Come on. We're going to the airport."

I just shake my head and chuckle. "I have to study."

"Study for what? You're the smartest girl I know. Plus, there is a special on tonight." He wiggles his thick brown eyebrows.

I could use a little distraction, and the airport is our place. We haven't gone in a while, and something about this fun side of Gannon I hadn't allowed myself to see in a while is spurring me on.

"Fine. But just for a little bit." I point a finger at him as I grab my purse to head out.

Gannon nods solemnly, like he'll be on his best behavior.

Two hours later, and I know that was a lie ... on both our parts.

We're lying on the hood of Gannon's car, just like we have been for an hour and a half. Just two months into our freshman year, we discovered the tiny offshoot dirt road that snakes out to the back of the Talcott Airport. Barely anyone knows about it, or at least we've never seen anyone else out here.

Before long, the airport, as we call it, became our spot here. The one we came to when we needed to get away or relax or just not think about everything for a while. The dirt road butts right up to the fence that keeps people out, right near the runway and on the flight path overhead.

And Gannon is right about tonight being special. They must be testing something, or just have a lot of flights scheduled, because we've had the roar of engines over our heads the entire night.

The hood of his car rattles as another mid-size plane shoots off into the night sky, the lights of its belly illuminating like twinkling stars as it grows farther and farther away.

"Thanks for suggesting this. It's been too long." I sigh, my whole being at peace.

"There is something that makes you and your problems feel so small out here." Gannon's voice is husky with the night air.

The dark surrounds us, and I'm perfectly aware of how close we have to lie to one another. He's a big guy, and with the way the hood slopes, we have to crowd toward the middle.

"It's true. I could afford a little big picture these days." Since my world feels about as tiny and hopeless as a thimble.

I feel him shift his head to look at me. "Everything is going to come up roses."

Gulping, all I can do is nod. Another plane throttles over us, and I watch in wonder as it races off. The adrenaline paired with the utter relaxation makes this activity a complete oxymoron, and I wouldn't trade it for the world.

Plus, the fact that this is *our* thing has always made it feel more special. Although, sometimes I wonder if Gannon has ever brought a girl out here.

"Dance with me." He hops off the hood, all of those lean limbs moving in a swagger that shouldn't be legal.

"I'm perfectly fine lying here." I grin up at the stars.

I don't like to dance outside of the studio or in front of anyone else. Plus, if Gannon holds me in his arms, it will lead to dangerous things.

We're in a good place. Since that impromptu social media shoot, our friendship is more jovial, if not glazing over the things we don't want to talk about. Our old camaraderie has returned, and neither of us are acknowledging the things that lie just beneath the surface.

"But I owe you one." Now he laces his fingers in mine, and like I knew it would, his touch paints tempting pictures.

"What do you mean?" My heart begins to thump, because he can't be talking about what I think he is.

"From prom. I was a jerk who ran out on you when I promised you a dance. Shit, I should have taken you myself in the first place."

When he asked some popular girl from our grade, I'd been devastated. I cried into my pillow for many nights leading up to what was supposed to be a monumental high school event. And then hearing from someone else that he and his popular crew had left before the last hour of the dance was underway ... it was crushing.

I swore that night that I'd get over my irrational crush. Yet, here I am, my heart completely melting as he says the simplest of things.

"Didn't think you remembered that," I murmur.

"I remember most everything when it comes to you." His eyes sear into mine.

I relent, letting him help me down off the car and coming to stand in front of him. His arms wrap around my waist, and I have to basically press up on my tiptoes to reach my arms around his neck. Every pore is on fire, so acutely aware of how he's holding me. My heart is jumping for joy, the giddy school girl who once dreamed of this moment is having it finally come true.

"And all my life, I prayed for someone like you. And I thank God, that I, that I finally found you ..." Gannon does his best K-Ci & JoJo impression.

If only he knew how desperately I used to play that song on my headphones, in my room, when I thought Aunt Cher was asleep. I'd look up at my ceiling and pray that someday, the boy I loved would love me back.

I need to change the subject, to stick to the plan that I told him we were following from the day I heard Aunt Cher was sick.

Just friends, no discussion of the night we blew each other's minds in my bedroom.

"Did you ever bring a girl out here? Besides me, of course." I press my cheek to his chest so I don't have to look him in the eyes when he answers.

"I would never do that." Gannon sounds offended. "You don't think much of me these days, huh?"

This is one moment I didn't want to have to talk. I wanted to dance to the sound of the crickets and the plane engines. But I can't help myself.

"You went on a TV show and told a woman you didn't know that you could see yourself marrying her."

Because that's the root of the problem. It's the incident that brought years of unspoken tension to a head.

He sways me back and forth. "I was a moron. It was all fake. I'm sorry. And I should have asked you to prom. I'm sorry I didn't. I'm sorry for a lot of things."

Being in Gannon's arms feels better than anything in the world. Knowing that he sees me in a way I've always wanted him to feels better than anything. But I feel like I'm teetering here, just about to take a nosedive when he lets me go after the novelty wears off.

"We should probably talk about us, huh?" he whispers, nuzzling my ear.

"Do we have to?" I'm scared.

At one point, I would have loved nothing more than for Gannon to want to talk about our relationship in a romantic way. Now? I'm terrified. What if he doesn't want a long-term thing? What if he won't commit? What if he leaves me?

I'll lose my best friend and gain a broken heart when I'm in no shape for either.

Sometimes, those closest to me tell me I'm too nice. That my kind nature gets in the way of what I want to say or express. Often, Gannon has told me that.

And it strikes again here. I've waited for this dance for a very long time, and I don't want to ruin it. Even though I feel like drudging up my baggage when it comes to him, I won't.

I'd rather forget it, gloss it over with niceness, and bask in the simple bliss of this night as airplanes fly over our heads.

"Oh my God, Gannon!"

A teenage girl shrieks, and so does her middle-aged mother beside her.

"Hey, how are you?" I put on my mega-watt camera smile.

The smile may be honed and perfected, but my appreciation for fans is always genuine. I would have nothing if it wasn't for them, and I'll always stop to chat.

"We can't wait for the panel!" The mom gives me heart eyes.

"Well, we can't wait to answer your questions. It should be a great time." I nod.

"Can we get a picture with you?" her daughter asks, holding out her iPhone.

My sister Quinn interrupts, "You're really not supposed to take pictures until the actual event ..."

I roll my eyes at her. "Excuse my sister. Of course, I'll take a picture."

The duo cozies up next to me as my sister wearily takes the girl's phone to snap a picture. After we're done taking the photo, they thank me profusely, and I think the mom wants to ask for my number, but Quinn shuttles me off. She knows when to interfere and do damage control.

We're in New York for a Right Kingdom event. That's what the fan base for the reality dating show I was on called themselves. They were obsessed with every contestant, couple, breakup, scandal, and more ... and it was blasted over multiple fan accounts all over social media.

"Does Mom know you're skipping school for this?" I ask out of concern for my sister's education, not her relationship with our mother.

The hotel and ballroom where the event is being held is this swanky boutique hotel in the city, and it's teaming with *Mr. Right* and *Mrs. Right* fans. I'm getting recognized left and right, and the boost to my ego feels good. Hopefully, there are some studio execs here today and we get some traction on a pilot or script ... or two.

"Do you think she'd even care if she knew?" Quinn snorts.

When the event producers said I could bring my agent for free, Quinn jumped at the chance. I tried to shut it down; I did not need my baby sister in a room full of New York City sharks and crazed fans, but she got the emails first and therefore booked two rooms.

Part of me is glad she's here, though. Over the past couple of months, she's learned the business way more than I had. I'm the pretty face, and she's the brains. Honestly, she could probably run circles around or eat the rest of these sharks. Growing up in a home where you had to hustle for attention, to eat, and grow up at a young age will do that to you.

"Probably not," I respond.

Quinn hasn't been super open about what's going on at home, but I have a feeling it's much of the same neglect I suffered through the years. I know she's holding down the fort, but an eighteen-year-old girl should not be the ward for four other kids.

Which is why I'm working so hard. Which is why I say yes to everything, including this fan event even though I'll have to drive back to college after dark tomorrow morning to make the classes I can't afford to miss.

The panel begins, and I'm seated next to a former Mrs. Right, not the one whose season I was on, two other male contestants from other seasons, and three female contestants who were all on *Mr. Right.*

The host, a guy who reminds me of a poor man's Ryan Seacrest, is rifling through audience questions. The former Mrs. Right gets asked about her fiancé, who she found on the show but isn't in attendance today. One of the other male contestants talks about his battle with addiction that was featured on the season.

Then it gets to me, and an audience member steps up to the mic.

"Gannon, we all want to know. Are you single?" The woman, who has to be ten to twenty years older than I am, has a mischievous twinkle in her eye.

I freeze. My mind goes blank, and then the only thing there is Amelie's face. A second goes by, and then another. I feel someone down the table staring at me, because I still haven't answered.

Then my gaze catches sight of Quinn, who looks like she's about to murder me, and I snap out of it.

"I'm currently on the market, but ... there might be someone special." I give her my most glowing smile.

An audible sigh and *aw* goes through the crowd. Always leave them guessing, that's what a producer on the show told me at the finale taping. If I could keep them hooked, keep them interested in my next move, I'd find a following in this business. And from that, I'd be able to launch the career I wanted.

The panel goes on for another hour, and then I sign autographs until my hand cramps up. I'm so appreciative of it all, but by the time Quinn and I are in the elevator headed upstairs for our rooms, I feel like I've sprinted a marathon.

"What's up with you? You seemed off out there." Quinn flops down on the queen bed in my room once we enter.

"Did I? Do you think the fans noticed?" I'd never want to come off as anything other than extremely professional to the event organizers.

Quinn shakes her head. "No one was the wiser. I just know you, you're the closest person to me in this world. So what's up?"

There is no use in hiding any more of this from Quinn. Knowing her, she'd probably hack my DMs or some shit. Not that she doesn't have access to everything already.

Plus, I need someone outside the situation to talk me straight again. To slap my head into a good space where I firmly know it's a bad idea to admit to my best friend that I'm in love with her.

"I slept with Amelie." I sigh, drumming my hands on the top of the mini-bar, debating whether I should pilfer a vodka or two.

My sister lets out a low whistle as she pops up, walks over, and rips open a bag of M&Ms from the box of pay-to-eat snacks. Guess there goes that expense.

"Long time coming, huh? Fucking finally." She chuckles.

"Wait, what?" Her reaction is not the one I was anticipating.

"What?" She stops, her expression confused, while she tosses a handful of chocolates into her mouth. "Was it a secret this whole time that you two were in love with each other? I thought we were all just waiting for you to get together."

"How do you know I'm in love with her?" I fire back, my guard going up.

I thought I'd hid my feelings so well.

"You literally went over to that girl's house in a blizzard once because she needed tampons. A seventeen-year-old guy stealing his mom's Playtex and driving on ice just to comfort a girl with uterus problems? Uh yeah, I knew you were head over heels after that moment."

I cock my head to the side. "*Huh.*"

"You guys should just make it official already. The rest of us are bored. Also, you deserve to be happy."

"We haven't exactly had the best role models when it comes to relationships," I grumble.

Quinn points at me, then circles her finger around. "Stop that. Stop all that. Don't let Mom have more control over you than she actually does. The woman doesn't even care about controlling you, so don't let her. She fucked up when it came to love, but you don't have to. Plus, look at who you picked to love. Amelie couldn't be more stable, more kind. Mom's choices have always been assholes, at best. You're in love with a girl who is way better than you. Which means you'll always be trying to prove yourself. That's a good thing."

Quinn's words hit me square in the heart.

Amelie is usually all I'm thinking about these days, but it's on overdrive after the other night at the airport. I had to leave about three days later, and when I get back to Talcott, she'll be gone taking care of Aunt Cher in Webton.

We need to talk, it's far past time, but I chickened out while we were dancing on that dirt road. Amelie wanted to avoid it, I know that, and the moment was so perfect that I let it happen, too.

Maybe my sister is right; I may not think I deserve Amelie, but I'd never hurt her because I'd spend my entire life trying to prove I'm worthy of a woman like her.

"I just got an email. Keith Wonderstone's people are here,

he's putting together a new show they can't talk about. But they want to talk to you about it." Quinn's frantic words interrupt my Amelie thoughts, and I see her head is now buried in her phone.

Keith Wonderstone is a bigwig for teen drama shows, and even some of the ones that Amelie and company like to binge on Netflix after a hangover. His name is synonymous with plucking undiscovered talent and turning them into franchise stars.

"Hell yes." I bounce my elbows up and down on my knees, pumped but trying to stay calm.

"I'll set up a lunch for us tomorrow before we leave." Quinn's fingers are flying over the screen as she taps out the email response.

If I could get in with Keith and his people, I could possibly book something. Which could lead to a paycheck, one that I could send home to Webton and help my brothers and sisters.

This trip, one I had to squeeze in for fear of missing college courses, has paid off. Even if we only get one sip of coffee with Keith, at least I know I'm on his radar.

Things might be working out, and I allow myself one breath of hope.

22

My five roommates and I stand in a huddle on the campus quad.

Around us, there are tons of groups made up of different off campus houses, dorm roommates, and suite-shares. Someone is yelling over a loudspeaker, and there is campy carnival music playing that hurts my ears.

"Why the hell are we here?" Bevan snarls.

If there is anyone who hates group activities more than quiet, bookworm me, it's Bevan. While she's ultra-competitive, group bonding is her hell.

And she also might want to kill Scott, who organized this whole thing, because he called the one person she hates more than group activities.

Callum is here because he has to be in order for us to win. Technically, he's still on the lease, even if he's crashing on a buddy's couch to avoid Bevan, his ex-girlfriend. Since Scott wants to win whatever prize it is that comes at the end of these relay races, he resorted to calling Callum. I think Bevan might murder him ... or both of them.

And to say that the tension and awkwardness between them

is affecting the group would be an understatement. Mostly, the sadness wafting off both of them is overwhelming. I know how upset Bevan has been, and Callum looks like shit. Their relationship is the kind that is more on and off than a light switch, and it was so toxic for both of them. Even though they love each other so much it hurts, that was the problem. They were always in pain.

"This would win us free coffee from the cafe for a month! Don't you all want that?" Scott looks at us like we're crazy.

"Wait, so free coffee is the thing you try hard for and are passionate about? I've seen you be apathetic at best about flunking out of that trig course, but this is what gets you hot and bothered?" Bevan is incredulous.

"I have a thing for those whipped girly lattes." He shrugs, then claps his hands. "All right team. I can definitely walk across the field on my hands, ninja style. Who is doing the piggy back leg, and who is going to do the scale the tree TikTok challenge?"

Gannon's hand shoots up. "Ams and I have got the scaling me challenge. I've seen it a billion times on TikTok, and Ams is the most flexible one we've got."

Everyone's eyes zoom in on me, and I go bright red. "Gannon ..."

He hears the embarrassment in my voice and laughs. "I don't mean like that. Although ..."

This time, I actually guffaw.

"God, I mean, because of her dance background. Get your heads out of the gutter, people!" Gannon admonishes all of us.

"Sure, that's what you meant." Scott winks at him.

Great. Does everyone know we had sex? I probably should have thought of that before this moment. I could have gone through the stages of embarrassment when I wasn't in front of all of my roommates.

"Enough of this," Taya snaps, and it's so unlike her that everyone swings their head her way.

She's glaring at Gannon, and I would not want to be on the receiving end of whatever she's thinking. Taya is the most level-headed, laid-back person I know. She doesn't get angry like Bevan or weepy like me. But if she's agitated, and right now she's bordering on furious, I'd steer way clear.

"Let's just get to it." She corrects her tone, coming off a little more like her normal self. "Bev and I will do the piggyback challenge, which leaves Callum as the other one walking across the field in a handstand."

"Ass backward? Sounds like him," Bevan mutters under her breath.

Callum's eyes go steely, but before he can say anything, a whistle blows.

"All right roomies, let's get to your relays!" the organizer calls out, a peppy girl with a high pony and a clipboard.

"She's definitely an RA." Gannon snorts as we walk side by side.

"You should know, didn't you screw ours freshman year?" We lived in the same dorm, and I swear he slept with the one on our floor.

I'm getting back at him for exposing our personal life back there, and we both know it.

"Sorry, shouldn't have made that comment." He hangs his head, deflated.

That guilty conscience of mine, which aches any time I'm not at my nicest, slams into me. "It's okay. You were just making a joke."

Now he gives me his signature grin, and my heart is back to melting. I'm having so many mixed emotions when it comes to him that I can hardly keep up.

"So what is it that we're doing here?"

Gannon pulls out his phone and clicks through some apps before coming to a video. A girl is legitimately scaling this guy, climbing him like a damn tree. My mouth drops open because I'm going to have to do that on Gannon, but I study it. I'm not one to let my friends down, and so if this is what I have to do to win Scott those damn coffees, I'll do it.

A familiar face catches my attention in the crowd, and I don't miss Jameson staring daggers at Gannon and me.

"Want me to beat the shit out of him?" Gannon puffs out his chest and throws an arm around me.

I shrug out of the hold and put my palm to his heart. "Don't you dare. He's mad for a completely valid reason."

Shame burns in my gut, because I hate that I hurt him.

"Fine, let's focus," Gannon grumbles, throwing one last searing look over his shoulder. "Should we practice?"

My heart kicks up a notch. I don't think I can do that twice, because I might pull a muscle. But more importantly, I'll never be able to do it a second time after I grope Gannon all over his body once.

"Nah. Let's not jinx it." I wave it off nonchalantly.

A couple minutes later, the student organizing our relay comes over and tells us to stand in a certain spot. Rules are explained about how if the person climbing falls off the stationary person, we'll be disqualified, and then we're at the ready.

Gannon offers me his hand and his thigh to propel myself up onto his body. Hesitantly, I grab it. Of course, I trust him, but trusting him like this only makes my heart fall further. Meanwhile, it's already in dangerous territory and always has been.

The whistles blows, and we're off at warp speed. For the duration of the relay, my mind is on conforming and twisting my body, straining my muscles around Gannon's so that I don't fall off. Every time I think I might, his hand is there to hold me up.

Each time I get stuck, he works in tandem, moving himself to give me room to perform.

Finally, I twist myself around to his front, so I'm essentially straddling him as he holds me in midair. Almost like he did the night on my desk.

Reality comes slamming up at me, like the ground just slapped my body, and I blink as we're nose to nose. Gannon is breathing heavy, but the interruption of someone yelling in our faces jolts us out of the haze we're in.

"These are our winners!" the student organizer cries, making a spectacle of us.

My cheeks, my heart, my stomach, the place between my thighs, they all burn bright red as Gannon slides me down his front. It's like he's moving me in slow motion so that I feel every ripple of his body, every divot I've never gotten a good look at in private.

Sometimes I wish we weren't in the dark the night we had sex. It's been a fantasy of mine to look at him, all of him, good and long and in the light.

"Look, Scott is about to fall on his face." Gannon breaks my eye contact but is still holding both of my arms by the elbow.

A rush of air expels from my lungs, and it's weird because I didn't think I was holding it.

We've been in neutral for the past couple of weeks, not wanting to rock the boat or confront what's going on. But it's clear after this that I can't go on with this *everything's normal* facade.

I have too many things going on; I don't need more drama or strife.

But part of me can't help but think, is it time to confess my feelings to Gannon once and for all?

"Stop fucking with Amelie."

Taya is in my room before I even invite her in, and I let out a huge sigh.

The last two weeks have been so hectic that I haven't even gotten to talk to Amelie like I want to. I had a plan to sit her down and hash this all out the moment she got back from Webton, but then Scott insisted on the field day and the whole house was within earshot. We needed a quiet, private space to dig deep into our issues and hopefully resolve them.

And even more hopefully, she'll listen when I tell her that I love her. Because no matter how much I keep trying to tell myself I don't deserve her, the universe, and even my sister want me to get the hell over myself.

But of course, Taya is here to smack me down to reality. "I love you, Tay. But it's none of your business."

"It is my business when you've been making googly eyes at her, leading her on, and now she's done with Jameson because of you. Jesus, Gannon, don't you know how long she's been waiting for this? I told you before you went to Webton for Cher that you had to stay away from her. You promised! I swear to God, Gannon—"

"You don't think I know?" My voice is quiet, shredded. "Of course, I know how she feels about me. I'm not as big of a moron as you guys think I am."

"What?" Taya's mouth drops open.

She shakes her head in disbelief, as if she can't imagine that I'm really saying this.

"I know how she feels about me. I've always known. Do you think it hasn't gutted me for eleven years? Do you think it feels good to turn my cheek every time she looks at me with that longing gaze? You think I don't want to kiss her every time she's upset, or every time she fucking breathes?"

My throat is ragged with the hurt I've been shoving back down for years. Taya looks like she could both kill me and burst into tears. I love her and Bevan, like sisters, but they've only been getting Amelie's side. I'm also an injured party here, forced to swallow the love I have for her. And I've had no one to talk to about it. Because if I voiced it, I might act on the feelings I was trying to ignore. That was my rationale, anyway.

"But why? Gannon, what the fuck? If you knew all this time, and you led her on like this—"

I think I pull a muscle in my neck I whip it so fast. "I never led her on. Don't you even say it. I've been here, as a friend, as her closest person. But I've never tried to trick her, or promise her things I can't give her. I've been a shoulder, but nothing more."

"Just by sticking around you've done that." There is sympathy in her voice, but also an edge of anger. "And let's not pretend you haven't been more. Not after you slept with her. What the hell did you think that would give her if it wasn't blinding and rose-colored hope?"

I run my fingers through my hair and then fist them,

relishing the bite of pain at my scalp. "I ... couldn't stay away. I should have, I know that. But ... she's my magnet. I'm drawn to her. I don't want to hurt her, I know I don't deserve her, but I can't help myself. I have to be near her."

"You don't deserve her?"

We're standing across the room from one another, and how confused Taya seems to be is palpable.

"I never have, isn't that what you always thought? I'm an asshole, just a charming face, no substance. My family never taught me to love. Amelie ... she's the definition of everything good. She's nice, angelic, beautiful both inside and out. She's the type of person no one can ever say a bad word about, and I'm the complete opposite. It's no mystery that everyone who knows us, our friendship, thinks that I'm the wolf and she's the naive Red Riding Hood. That one day, I'll eat her and spit her back out. It's why I've stayed away. Why I've put on the facade and worn my reputation, or the one people gave me, like a suit of armor. You don't think I love her exactly the way she loves me? Then I've been doing a hell of an acting job."

Exhaustion seeps from my pores. I rub my forehead in frustration and depletion. Keeping it all inside this long has made me a shell of a man.

"I can't believe you," Taya growls. "All this time you claim you love her, and you've let her suffer through that crush? I don't care if you think you didn't deserve her! You let Am hang on your every move while you felt the same about her? What is wrong with you?"

"So, I'm damned if I do, damned if I don't? Perfect." I grit my teeth.

Taya takes two deep breaths. "Shit, I ... I'm just worked up. I don't understand why two people who love each other have waited so long to actually admit it. Especially with all she's going through."

"Like you admitted you had a gigantic crush on Austin in high school?" I raise an eyebrow at her.

Yeah, of course, I know about the Austin crush. For one, Amelie tells me most everything. And second, I was in planning sessions with the girls around the time of that sophomore homecoming dance he finally noticed Taya. They would ask me how she should proceed, if she should throw herself at him, etc.

"Touché, asshole. But ... touché. Things worked out for us in the end. That could happen for you and Amelie."

"One second, you're telling me to stay the fuck away from her, and now you want our happily ever after?" I cock my head to the side.

Taya shrugs. "I want everyone to have the love I have. And I know how badly Amelie has wanted that with you."

"We've done everything backward. I'm not sure there is any way to correct it."

"Then why don't you start at the beginning? Actually talk to her."

Her advice goes off like a lightbulb in my brain, and I start toward the day. "Thanks, Tay!"

"What, *now*?" I hear her say as I take the stairs down two at a time.

I've been trying to convince myself for weeks that I need to just confront Amelie with everything. Her best friend coming to me has spurred me to do so, and I'm not losing this momentum.

Which is why I burst into Amelie's room and plan to do just that.

Books are scattered about my bed, my eyes narrowed at them as I try to pick which one to choose next.

I'm taking a paranormal literature course, and while it's fascinating, I have a hard time getting into the mystical and magical. I'm much more comfortable in a women's fiction genre or with a good regency romance, heck, I'll even take an interesting autobiography. Something about my brain makes it hard to immerse myself in worlds that might not conform to reality.

Which is why I took the course, I'm trying to get better at it. As a librarian, I want to be able to make impactful recommendations in each corner of the book world.

While I'm tapping my chin, contemplating the ten books I checked out of the library, Gannon storms in.

"We're going to have this talk, right here, and right now."

He practically stamps his foot as he points to the floor, as if to say I better come stand over there to talk to him.

I stay seated on my bed, more than surprised. "Um, what?"

"I'm tired of skirting around this, of never talking about what happened between us. Or, fuck, let's face it, has been happening between us for eleven years. Everybody wants to have their own damn opinion and I'm not allowed to voice mine for fear of upsetting you more or breaking my own rules or whatever the hell else is holding us back. We're talking. Now."

Oh, *shit*. He's really aggravated and I wonder what got him to this point. But I don't have time to think about that because my mind is going into panic mode. I don't want to have this talk. I don't want to expose all of the scary, painful parts of myself. I don't want him to know that I've been in love with him since the first moment I saw him in the fifth grade.

"Gannon, we really don't have to. I told you, we're good. I care so much about you, we're best friends—"

Forget everything I said after the field day this afternoon. I'm too much of a coward to confront him, to tell him everything I've felt for him all these years. I'm that scared, kind little girl who never wants to feel anything too big.

"Bullshit, we're best friends. Best friends don't fuck each other's brains out. Best friends don't think twenty-four seven about what you sound like orgasming on my cock. Best friends don't wish they could be holding you every night as they fall asleep. Best friends aren't so fucking in love with you that I can't eat, can't sleep, can't fucking function because you don't know how much I love you."

I swear to you, my stomach falls out of my butt and through the levels of this house. That's how shocked I am. He's in fucking love with me?

Gannon is covering his mouth like he didn't mean to say that. Or at least not right now.

"You don't mean that," I blurt out because I truly almost can't believe it.

This is everything I've ever wanted to hear, and my mind has to be playing tricks on me.

He blinks, seeming to come out of the shock that he just

admitted that. Then nods his beautiful damn head, reassuring both himself and me.

"Yes, I absolutely do. I am in love with you. I have been for a very long time. You want to know why I'd always rip on the guys who noticed you or the ones you deemed worthy of dating? None of those guys were good enough for you because they're. Not. Me." Gannon pounds his chest, exaggerating each word.

This is where my temper comes out. It's so extremely rare that I never know when it will make an appearance. But when it does, I can't control a lick of it. Part of me is rebelling the idea that Gannon is telling me he loves me. My brain is rattled by the last few months, and it doesn't seem real that something I've been wanting and wishing for so long is actually coming true. And while that part wants to accept it, is giddy by the prospect of it ...

The other part of me is angry. How could he let me go this long thinking he only saw me as his little sister? His friend? If what he's saying is true, that he's sabotaging my dating life because he's always loved me? It makes me downright furious.

Jabbing my finger out in the air toward him, my tone is bitter. "You? The guy who has watched from right beside me as I pined after him for years? Who never even gave me a shot and made me feel like some unattractive kid sister? The guy who left me to go to Hollywood and make out with some random chick, then tell her he might marry her? Yeah, that sounds like someone I deserve. That sounds like someone worthy of my time."

Gannon flounders, his mouth opening and closing several times before he gets words out. "Ams, please, you have to listen to me. To believe me. For so long, I thought exactly that. I was never worthy of you. I'm still not. But I can't sit here and watch you hurt over Aunt Cher, be able to hold you, know what it feels like to be inside you, and hold back any longer. The possibility that you could fall in love with someone else? It makes me nauseous. Being with you through Cherry's stuff has shown me just how much I don't want to lose you. All of that Hollywood shit? It's bullshit. You know me, Ams. You're the only one who has ever truly seen me. I may not be good enough for you, but I swear I'm going to try every second moving forward to show you that I am. Because I love you more than I love myself. I used to think that meant letting you go, but I'm too selfish. I'm in too deep. I want you. I need you."

Tears leak down my cheeks. How could they not? He's saying things only dream-world Gannon has ever said to me.

"I was there, Gannon, right freaking there. I was this close to being over you, to putting it behind me! And it's like you knew that and started messing with my heart. You couldn't just let me be happy? You couldn't just let me get over you, move on with someone who I had no baggage or past drama with? God, I could hate you for that."

He moves to me now, cupping my face with his hands. "I'm sorry. I'm so sorry, Ams. I was trying to spare you any pain, but I can see now what an idiotic plan I've had. I should have taken you to prom. I should have asked you to be my girlfriend all the way back in middle school when I used to have wet dreams over your boobs. I should have been the guy to move you into your college dorm freshman year and then stay the night in our first grownup, no parent home. I hate that I was so blind and misguided. But I'm telling you now, I have always loved you. I love you so much that when I look at you, my body convulses like it's short circuiting. Like, without you, I won't be able to function."

I might have KO'd right there. There might be an Amelie-sized hole in my floorboards because I've physically dropped six feet under. Stunned isn't even the right word. Gobsmacked. Hit by a tractor-trailer. Those don't even seem to encompass the pure, raw, unfiltered shock I'm feeling.

Those three little words finally seem to sink in. Gannon Raferty is in love with me. How long I've been waiting for them, how long I've dreamed of this.

And how I wish I could take them at face value. How I wish this was like a movie, where I wept and we hugged and the title credits rolled. Where I knew, without a doubt, that these feelings were real and we'd ride off into the sunset.

But my caution is supplant, and has been for so long when it comes to him. I learned not to put weight into his promises. I learned never to get my hopes up. So now that he's fulfilled my highest ones, I'm not sure how to react.

I'm not sure if my vocal cords even work at this point, and I think Gannon misinterprets it. He takes it as me fluttering my lashes, becoming woozy with romance, overwhelmed in my girlish way with my emotions.

Which is why he goes in for a kiss. His eyes are pained and ravenous before I shut mine and can't see them anymore. Because what he's doing to my mouth is simply too exquisite to use any other body part or sense.

His kiss is urgent, breathless, and literally makes my knees weak. They buckle with each stroke of his tongue. I can't help but get caught up in it, giving myself to his passion and meeting him in the middle. This kiss puts fire in my veins, the kind no boy has ever been able to compare to.

"I love you ... I love you ... I love you ..." he chants between each kiss, as if he's been holding it in for so long that it's painful not to let it out now.

"I need ... space." I breathe, even though there is no air in my lungs.

I'm trying to process way too many emotions, and it honestly feels like I am about to have a breakdown. I'm constantly worried about Aunt Cher, and then I'll stumble into how much I love Gannon, only to trip out of that and be furious for the way he portrayed himself on TV. Then I'll feel terrible for how I ended things with Jameson and feel shame that I did it for Gannon without knowing if his intentions were true and long-lasting. Then the train of thought about school and chemo and my internship will pull in, and it's off to the anxiety races.

This conversation has needed to happen for weeks, and now I can't bring myself to talk. Gannon spilled his guts all over me, when what I need is to dissect every part of our relationship so that I can make a decision.

Taya and Bevan are typically the logical ones, and I play the game of life with my heart. But that strategy has burned me so many times when it comes to Gannon that I find I need air.

I need time.

Gannon is pacing in front of me, running his hands through his hair. "Okay, okay. I can leave you alone. Can I come check on you tonight?"

For the first time in our entire lives together, I don't want to see him. It's an oxymoron; the minute he confesses he loves me, I can't stand to be in his presence. But it's about self-preservation. If I'm going to do this, detail the whole epic journey of how I came to love him and what this leap of faith means, then I need to at least take a beat.

"No. I need space, for however long I need it. When I'm ready, I'll come to you."

I'm not exaggerating when I say my best friend, the boy I love who I now know loves me, looks confused. No one has ever said no to him. And not even that, he's just never been in a situation where he doesn't get his way.

"I love you, Ams."

Each word is both a caress and an uppercut to the heart. I have no idea why I'm reacting this way, but I'm serious in knowing that I need to distance myself from him right now.

Gannon backs out of my room but never breaks eye contact until he closes the door.

For the first time since I got the news about Aunt Cher's cancer, I'm packing my bags in anticipation of going to Webton. Even with chemo and all of the scary medical words, I need to be home in her arms.

She'll know what to do. About everything.

"Honestly, if you close your eyes and don't acknowledge the poison flowing through my veins, this could be the spa."

Aunt Cher cracks the sick joke, and a couple of the chemo patients around us chuckle and nod their agreement.

"Did you want me to put cucumber slices on your eyes?" I play along.

"No, I'd rather eat them. But I could go for a nice pedicure."

"I'll bring nail polish next time," I say, only half-kidding.

Whatever she wants me to do while she sits there being pumped full of cancer drugs, I'll do. Currently, we're reading trashy tabloids and sucking on ice pops. I also have Mancala in my oversized tote, a Kindle loaded with her favorite books, and an eye mask in case she wants to try and sleep.

Thanksgiving is this week, but being that this is a chemo week for Aunt Cher, I get to be home with her for fourteen glorious days. Okay, so maybe they won't be glorious, but at least I have two weeks with her and it's a holiday. Granted, it will only be the two of us and I have to attempt to make the turkey because she's too weak.

Regardless of all the drawbacks, I'm happy that she's here with me this Thanksgiving. I can be thankful that my aunt is still smiling and cracking jokes. I can be thankful that we'll be in our warm home, with delicious food ... hopefully. Actually, I'm kind of excited to make the feast this year. I like to cook and bake, so doing so for Aunt Cher will be fun.

A male nurse comes to check on her IV line and examines the bag dripping into her arm.

"Figures I'd fall for the guy shooting poison into my arm." Aunt Cher bats her eyelashes, or what she has left of them, up at the nurse.

He's good-looking, with a head full of auburn hair and seriously gorgeous green eyes.

And he's looking at my aunt like he might want to ask her on a date, even though she's struggling to kick cancer's ass.

"You're shameless, Cher." He shakes his head and laughs under his breath.

I even think he might be blushing. It's clear he's smitten but trying to remain professional. Which is made worse when she says, "I'm simply trying to tell you that your ass looks *so* good in those scrub pants."

Hottie nurse shuffles away with bright red cheeks and a grin on his face.

"What is wrong with you?" I laugh-hiss.

She shrugs. "I could be dying. I have to shamelessly flirt with any guy I think is cute."

Hearing her say the word *dying* is like taking a machete to the heart. I turn my head so she can't see my face. I know she likes to make light of her cancer, that it's a way for her to cope. But for me, it slices deep every time. I can't tell her not to do it, but I also need a minute every time she makes a joke.

"What else is new? Let's talk about something normal for once." She sighs as if she's so over her cancer treatments.

I tap my chin, my heart pounding. I've barely burdened her with my life in the past few months, and a regular aunt-niece talk sounds nice. But there is something I've been dying to get her opinion on.

"I submitted my application for the New York Public Library. Oh, and not a big thing really, but Gannon told me he's in love with me."

Aunt Cher looks up from her trashy celebrity news magazine and blinks. "Well, I'm so happy you applied. When do you find out?"

"Christmas." I nod, every fiber of my being hoping she addresses the other thing I said.

"When it comes to Gannon, I'm glad the boy finally said what we all knew."

"What?" I shout, and heads turn our way.

One of the nurses, not the hottie who was flirting with my aunt, gives me a stern glance.

Sorry, I mouth to everyone in the room. "What do you mean 'what we all knew'? You've been telling me for years to stop crushing on him because he didn't deserve my heart and I could find someone better."

Aunt Cher shrugs. "Well, at first, I honestly did think that. That boy was a little shit coming over to my house in the early years. And your dad was so skeptical when you became best friends. Thought the boy would break your heart one day."

"Dad said that?" My heart physically aches.

It's not often that we talk about my parents. It just hurts too much, and while we've both made some peace, bringing them up, even the good times, makes me want to shrink away from the world. I can't imagine what it's like for Aunt Cher. My mom was her best friend, they spent decades together, and her life changed when she became my guardian. I know it's extremely difficult for her, too.

She nods profusely. "He loved Gannon, don't get me wrong. Once we all figured out what was going on in his home life, we really felt for him. But your daddy saw the way you looked at him. He saw that growth spurt Gannon had the year after you guys met. 'Nothing but trouble' he'd shake his head and say."

Aunt Cher and I chuckle because my dad was pretty much spot-on. And my heart warms because I know my parents loved Gannon. It's part of the reason I love him so much … because he knew them and I knew how he was with them. Of course, I love him as a person and a man, but he will always have a leg up on other guys I might date. Because he knew me when I was their daughter.

"Part of me always wanted it to be Gannon, because he knew my parents so well. That was definitely part of why I was so blindly in love with him. Once my parents were gone, it's like anyone I meet from here on out will never know them. I won't have my mom's stamp of approval, my dad won't get to grill him before he takes me on a date. If I ended up with someone who actually knew them, and knew them so well, then that erased a little bit of the hurt that I would feel on those big days. I won't get to have my dad walk me down the aisle, but if I'm walking toward a man I know he loved like a son, that would make things a little easier."

Aunt Cher nods like this makes all the sense in the world.

"So all those years of you telling me to find someone who was worthy of my love?" I level her with a hard stare.

Aunt Cher does have the decency to look a little guilty, but her upper lip is stiff.

"I was supposed to be taking care of you. I saw how lovesick you were over Gannon, and that boy had a lot of growing up to do. I thought I was telling you what was best at the time. Of course, I could see how he felt, but he never wanted to admit that to himself. It would only have caused you more hurt to know that he felt that way about you, or pining after it when he wasn't ready."

"And now that he says he is?" I have to know what she thinks.

If my aunt doesn't think I should be with him or that we won't be good together, it will heavily sway my decision. Part of me needed some space specifically so I could come talk to her about it. In a way, I doubted my heart and my head when it comes to Gannon now. I've been wrong so many times about him that I needed the sagest person in my life to ensure I'm going down the right path.

"I think that Gannon loves you more than one human could possibly love another. I think he's flawed, and some of his priorities are out of whack, but that boy cares about you. He has always gone above and beyond to notice your feelings or be a friend. And well, I know how you feel about him. Only you know how ready he is. Only you can take the risk of falling completely in love with him. Hey, it doesn't hurt that he's an objectively gorgeous specimen, and that's not creepy it's just the truth."

She sticks her tongue out at me, and I flush. I mean, she's not wrong.

"But if it feels right in your heart, if you're willing to take the jump and hope you guys land together, then I'm all for it. If I've learned one thing over the past few months, it's that life is too short. I think you've been waiting a long while to give yourself permission to love and be loved by that boy. He's giving you the chance. Take it, and then give him a chance back."

I take a minute to consider her words, to really digest them. And when I'm done chewing them over, I reach out and thread my fingers through hers.

"So, you think I should ask the nurse out? I mean, it may be the last bang of my life." She wiggles her eyebrows at me.

"I'm equally horrified and impressed. And ... it's morbid AF, but I appreciate the effort." I give her a high five.

The hot male nurse must hear the slap of our hands because he looks over and smirks at Aunt Cher. Even with no eyebrows, an IV in her arm, and nausea plaguing her, Cher is still the brightest light in any room she occupies.

Universe, you can't take her. She's not ready yet. And what my boss bitch aunt says, goes.

S o I kind of threw up on her.

I've dreamed about the day I finally got to tell Amelie I was in love with her so many times. I'd make it romantic, special. I would speak in poems and bring gifts and then lay her down and finally show her, with our bodies, how much I've wanted her all along.

Well, I fucked her at a loud party, after being an absent asshole for months before, and then hemmed and hawed about telling her how I felt. And when I finally did, I basically attacked her with my words.

I was way too intense; I know it. But honestly? I never expected her to react the way she did.

Every sign I've gotten from her is that she's just been waiting for me to tell her I love her. That makes me sound like an asshole, but like I've said before, I was not doing so simply because I didn't believe I deserved her. I still don't, but I can't fight this any longer. If I fail, I fail. But at least she knows now.

It kills me that I'm back in Webton, where she's spending her Thanksgiving holiday, and she wants nothing to do with me. I haven't heard from or seen Amelie since the night I told her I'm in love with her. She spent one more day at our off-campus house before running back to Webton for Aunt Cher. And I'm guessing, a hiding place.

Maybe another guy would have texted her, called endlessly, sent flowers. But I know Ams was serious when she said she'd come to me. She'd be mad if I swayed her decision.

So I'm, metaphorically, standing stock-still. I'm ignoring fight-or-flight. I'm not moving a muscle for fear that she'll reject me, but also in hopes that she'll come back and tell me she's in love with me, too.

Doesn't mean it's not killing me, though. I'm in quiet agony, where any reminder of her sends a shock straight to my heart. And in our hometown, there are endless reminders. My driveway where we'd first smoked a cigarette and Amelie had coughed up a lung. The trail around the youth baseball fields where we'd sneak out and look at the stars. The high school where I'd walk next to her after every class, knowing I'd never be good enough to wrap an arm around her shoulder and have her call me her boyfriend.

Inside, my heart is bleeding. I don't know what I'll do if Ams says she doesn't want to be with me. That she doesn't want to take the risk of *us*. My heart will never belong to another girl, and I'll spend forever mourning what could have been.

That sounds dramatic, but it's true. Now that I've been completely honest with myself and her, I know there will never be anyone else for me.

My nerves rattle around in my body as I contemplate what will happen if she rejects me.

When I walk into the kitchen, three of my five siblings are seated at various places. Mallory is perched on the counter, scrolling rapidly through her cell phone. Fiona is at the kitchen table, doing what looks to be some schoolwork. And Fitz, my baby brother, is on the floor putting together a LEGO replica of a war plane.

"Does anyone clean up around here?" I eye the stack of dishes in the sink.

Being back in this house for the Thanksgiving holiday is less than desirable, but what was I supposed to do? If I didn't facilitate it, my brothers and sisters would have no turkey spread or any kind of merriment. Lord knows, my mother hasn't cooked food for us in years.

It's why I came home. A lot of times, I'll just stay at school for holidays or crash with a friend. Last year for Thanksgiving, I spent it with Aunt Cher and Amelie. But I feel guilty being gone for so long while filming the reality show, and from Quinn's description, things here aren't going great. Which is why I'm torturing myself with a week in my familial home.

Mallory, my second sister, raises her eyebrow and then rolls irises the same color as mine. "Quinn usually does it, but obviously she ain't here."

Quinn is out with her friends and a boyfriend, according to Mallory. We'd be having a talk about that when she got home, because I had no clue and I don't need my sister running around with fuckheads.

"Do we have any snacks?" Alwin, my middle brother, traipses into the kitchen in nothing but his athletic shorts.

"It's freezing outside, can you put some clothes on?" Fiona snarls.

Fi is the feistiest of us. She's probably been neglected the most as the third girl but not the baby. She's also going through puberty and doing it pretty much on her own. Sure, Mallory is here to help but Quinn is busy with senior year and being my agent, while Mom is nowhere in sight.

Honest to God, I haven't seen my mother once since I've been home. She could be on a bender, or a gambling trip, or holing up with the next guy she's plotting to make her meal ticket. It's better that she's not here, so we can at least have some drama-free time together and maybe even a decent holiday.

Mom in the mix means her ego, narcissism, and deep-rooted issues take up all the air in the room. We'd have to hear her constantly banging on about how she sacrificed her life to raise us. How we are ungrateful brats. How we've taken her money and her good looks. How she wishes she was still free to go out and do whatever she wanted.

As if she's not doing so now, nor has she done it since I was weaned from breastmilk. Can you hear my huge eye roll?

I'm not even affected by her anymore, I've had years of becoming desensitized and unemotional when it comes to my mother. But some of my siblings don't know what's good for them yet.

"Fuck off," Alwin shoots back at Fiona.

"Language!" I hiss at him, pointing to Fitz sitting on the floor.

My brother grumbles something under his breath and flings open the pantry door to scrounge for something to eat.

I kneel down next to Fitz and pick up some LEGOS. "Need help, bud?"

He nods vigorously, clearly ecstatic that someone wants to play with him. "This is an actual B-52 bomber! Just like they had in World War II."

"Why does he even know what that war is?" Mallory cocks her head to the side.

It's a good question, considering the kid is barely at a second-grade reading level. He's smart as hell, but being that he is the youngest of six ... he hasn't gotten the help he's needed.

Fitz is the baby and acts as such. He's been late to do most everything, and not because our mother coddled him. But because he was raised by us kids, and we knew jack shit about parenting a child. But we banded together to give him the best life we could, and he's a sweet kid.

But he needs more, I know that. It's why I'm trying so hard to make it. I may not be able to be here or do things for him, but if I make enough money, I can hire someone to.

I ended up having that lunch meeting in New York City with Keith Wonderstone, and it went well. The guy is a little zany, but I'll hand it to him that he's a complete genius. He sees the entertainment industry and television space in a way no one ever could. I feel honored to be on his radar.

At the lunch, he asked me my sizes, my goals and what I *wouldn't* be willing to do. Is it sad I've gotten used to those types of questions from people in this industry? Asking someone's weight is as common as asking them their mother's or father's names.

Keith said he was interested in having me test with some other actors he was considering for a script he was pitching to a streaming service. It was a big one, and if he got a deal signed, the show was going to be huge. I knew it, and obviously so did he.

I left the meetings with high hopes, because we seemed to get along well enough and he seemed impressed by what I said I wanted to do.

But since then? Crickets.

Yes, I still get weekly ad revenue and Instagram brands wanting to partner with me. Which is great, considering it's an income source and I can send some of that to Quinn to help my brothers and sisters out. But I want something meaty, something that will help me make a name. I want the challenge of memorizing lines and becoming a character. I want to work with other up-and-coming talent.

I want to star in a breakout show and give everyone who ever doubted me the metaphorical finger.

Pushing those thoughts out of my head, I regard my brothers and sisters.

"You guys want to watch a movie?" I pose the question, knowing they need a little TLC.

"Can we watch *American Pie*?" Alwin looks hopeful.

"Absolutely not." I know exactly what he's hoping to see in that movie. And I know it because I was a horny teenage boy at one point.

"What about *Finding Nemo*?" Fitz's voice is meek because he probably thinks he'll be shot down.

"That movie is for babies!" Fiona growls.

"Hey." I give her a stern look. "I love *Finding Nemo*. But what if we watched ... *Mrs. Doubtfire*?"

It's a kid-friendly movie that the older ones would also find funny, and it's my last resort right now.

"Yeah, okay, I could do that." Mallory shrugs. "I'll make the popcorn."

"If we're having popcorn, I guess I'll stay for that corny movie." Alwin rolls his eyes.

"I like when he puts pie on his face!" Fitz giggles.

My siblings and I have never been super close, mostly because we were trying to survive and fend for ourselves. But as we assemble on the couch in the living room, my heart seizes with comfort. These are my people, no matter how strained things have been or will continue to be.

At least I can spend some time with my family while Amelie is taking her space.

But I do wonder when I'll finally feel like my life isn't always up in the air? When will my feet, and my goals, be firmly planted on the ground?

"I really have no idea why I let you talk me into this."

Someone is breathing on me, a kid who peed his pants in fourth grade is up on stage drunkenly singing a Pink Floyd song, and Bevan is way too drunk for me right now.

"Because Thanksgiving Eve is a rite of passage." Taya rolls her eyes at me.

It's the first year we're able to legally come to the bar to participate in what is always lauded as "college homecoming." Thanksgiving Eve is the night that every local kid who has gone off to college comes home, packs into the jankiest bar in town, and proceeds to get wasted. Then, most either fight with the people who bullied them, hook up with the guy they had a crush on back in high school, or puke all over their friend's childhood bedroom.

And okay, I'm technically not twenty-one yet. But when you're one-third of a hot girl crew, and at least one of us, Bevan, has a legitimate ID, the bouncers kind of don't care.

"I'm so not up for this," I murmur.

"Me either, it's why I'm doing shots!" Bevan jumps up and

down, her boobs jumping out of her tight black tank and black leather jacket.

"Easy, killer." Taya yanks the fifth shot of tequila out of our friend's hand. "Why do I know this night is going to end with her head in a toilet?"

That's said to me, and I shrug. "It probably will. But at least it won't be with her tongue in Callum's mouth."

"Always looking at the bright side, my friend." Taya chuckles.

I'm sure Callum is around here somewhere, as he went to our high school, too. It's probably why Bevan is getting shit-faced; she imagined our first time at a Thanksgiving Eve party would be with him. They are the ultimate high school sweethearts, everyone in Webton knows they're the golden couple. I mean, everyone who doesn't know them intimately. Everyone who does, knows they're a train wreck and always were. But still, this can't feel great for Bev; she had a vision of walking in here on a high horse, and now she's just at the bottom of a tequila bottle.

"I'll take that." I point to the shot, because I could use some liquid courage.

"Nervous about that?" Taya asks, tipping her head toward the back corner of the bar.

Big Joe's, the bar we're at, is packed to the gills. It's the place you go to get a drink with high school friends when you're home from college and where it's tradition to celebrate Thanksgiving Eve in Webton. It's the place that people who peaked in high school and like to think they're cool come to get loaded and brag about the glory days. The space is basically just a big warehouse stuffed with black wooden chairs and shiny silver tables. The bar is right in the center, a rectangle, with access on every side. And up front there is a stage and a dance floor, which are becoming rowdier by the second.

The whole place smells like liquor, the floor is sticky, and bad decisions are definitely being made.

Case in point, the liquor that burns my throat as it slides down. I grimace, nodding my head to the thing Taya is pointing at.

Gannon is across the bar, and he hasn't stopped staring at me since he arrived about half an hour ago. In a chambray button-down and olive-colored jeans, he looks like the epitome of a Thanksgiving feast. He's had a haircut since I last saw him, and my fingers itch to touch the closely shaved sides of his gorgeous head. What isn't closely shaved is his beard—it's practically a full one, which I never see on him.

Naturally, it's the hottest he's ever looked. Tall and towering over the crowd, he's impossible to ignore, try as I might.

Since my conversation with Aunt Cher, I've been trying to summon the courage to talk to him. To tell him that I want to leap over the edge with him. Of course, I'm head over heels in love with him, and now that I know how my aunt feels, and how my father felt, it gives me that last oomph I needed.

Plus, the space was good. It let me get my head on straight. I am in love with him, and I want him to know it.

But I'm so scared. Uttering those words has only ever been a fever dream, and now that I can do it and have him accept them so easily? It seems like I'm waiting for the other shoe to drop.

"It's a zoo in here," Austin, Taya's boyfriend, laments as he pushes through the crowd to rejoin our trio.

"No. It's you and who you are, which means you were probably stopped seventeen times to and from the bathroom." Bevan cackles.

Austin was hesitant to come back to Webton. He's a Van Hewitt, and they basically own this town. Bevan isn't kidding when she says that the Van Hewitt's are idolized in our hometown, and Austin is their king. Or was. After shirking the responsibility of coming home after he graduated college and taking over the family business, his family all but ex-communicated him. The feeling was mutual and allowed him to follow his dream of working as a radio personality in New York City.

I know he wants to spend the holiday with Taya, but running into one of his cousins at this bar or his father on the street was cause for concern. I'm glad he sucked it up and decided to come and stay with Taya and her family.

Taya is no stranger to family drama either. She and her family have been through it, but they've been healing and are closer than ever.

I'm so happy for both of them and kind of look at her and Austin like my love role models. They had to wade through a lot of baggage and some drama to end up completely in love.

Maybe I can do that, too ... with another shot of tequila.

I refrain, mostly because I'm trying to stop Bevan from breaking free and running onto the dance floor to twerk. I love my best friend, but she can't dance for shit.

Gannon is leaning against the wall, some of his old high school friends loitering around, trying to show off for him. He was always too cool, even for the cool crowd. I remember guys trying to emulate or outdo him and girls trying to get his attention in the most obvious of ways. Most of the time, he was oblivious. Gannon has the kind of swagger and effortless suaveness that couldn't be taught or replicated.

Sam, the guy we graduated with who was voted Most Likely to Get Busted for Growing Weed, is talking Gannon's ear off. He's leaning against the wall just like my best friend, except he doesn't look quite as cool doing it. Gannon, when we were on good terms, told me all about how most of the kids he hung out with in high school reached out to leach off him when he was on the season of *Mrs. Right*.

His eyes are pinned to me, and I suddenly feel naked under his gaze. It's been a week since he left my room to give me space.

And of course, each night I've dreamed of him telling me he loves me. Honestly, it's been on my mind every second of every day. I could melt over the way his eyes held me at that moment.

"Are you going to go over there or what?" Bevan interrupts my thoughts, sounding like she might just shove me across the room.

"I don't know." I sip my glass of white wine.

Well, more like chug. I can already feel the buzz in my veins, and I should slow down. This is only my first glass, plus that shot, but I'm trying to work up the bravery to go up to Gannon.

When I glance over again, he's moved off the wall in my direction. But he's standing his ground. He meant what he said about giving me space, and he knows me too well. He knows I wouldn't want him to push me or make the first move when I said I'd do so.

Gulping, I scoot off the barstool I'm occupying and pull up my big girl panties. Then, I begin my slow walk over to him.

"You came with them?" I point to Gia, his prom date from way back when, when I finally reach him.

Jealousy burns in my gut, both seeing how much of a knockout she is now and remembering how he left with her all those years ago. Gia is as gorgeous as ever, but there is something worn out about her. Last I'd heard, she'd been kicked out of college when she got caught dealing drugs, and is now living at home.

"I came alone. To see you. They just found me."

His honesty and the unnerving way his eyes are undressing me has electric sparks shooting down my spine and pooling between my thighs. There is something in the air tonight between us. Call it a reckoning. Say that the cup runneth over with sexual tension.

Either way, it feels like we're at a tipping point.

"Dance with me." Gannon interrupts the discussion I was

just about to launch into.

I realize, as my breath is stolen by the moment, that the DJ is playing our song. Well, one of them. Over the years, we've labeled a ton of songs as ours. But this one feels special.

"*Sangria*" by Blake Shelton courses over the room, the sexy ballad crooning into everyone's veins and taking the sexual tension all around us up a notch. Gannon and I coined this one ours after my first time getting truly drunk. It was at a house party where someone had supplied tubs of their mother's sangria recipe. Gannon practically had to carry me to his car, and he was driving by himself on a learner's permit. I told him he looked so beautiful that night, in my idiotic drunken stupor. He took me to the McDonald's drive-through, and we ate McFlurrys in the parking lot. It was one of the best nights of my life.

"Did you ask them to play this?" I whisper, his hand now on my back as he escorts me to the dance floor.

Gannon nods, and before I know what's happening, we're in the middle of the floor pressed against each other.

"I've been waiting all night to touch you. Hell, I've been dying for over a week just to see you in person." His voice hints at the desperation beneath.

I had this whole plan of talking to him, maybe acting friendly, or even seeing if he'd like to go outside and talk. But per usual, Gannon wrecks all my plans. One look at him, one word, and I'm under his spell. That charm invades my system, paralyzing me, and I'm a goner.

Is this what I'm afraid of? Fully falling for him? Because once I do, I know I'll never be able to crawl out of it if it ends badly.

Gannon's body gyrates against me as those big hands run down my sides. The song isn't slow exactly, but it's sex in lyrical form. Rhythmic and enchanting, dripping with lustful undertones and a grizzled bedroom voice. It's not a typical song for Blake, which makes it all that much more surprising.

"I love you." He bends, his teeth centimeters from the lobe of my ear.

The way he's holding me coupled with the way he sighs the endearment ... my knees actually buckle.

"Whoa there." He catches me, and I turn sheepishly into him.

"I'm not sure I'll ever get used to hearing that," I admit.

"Because you don't like it?" Gannon dips to get on my eye level, his whiskey pools warring between hope and panic.

My arms wind around his neck. "Because I've dreamed about it for so long, and now I don't think I could stand it if you stop."

A genuine expression of relief washes over his face, like I just broke his fever or made it possible for him to take a deep breath for the first time in months.

I hear people whispering around us. They're used to seeing Gannon and Amelie as best friends. Not this version of us where Gannon's hands are in very sensitive places on my body and his mouth is ghosting over the skin of my neck.

Suddenly, I don't feel much like dancing anymore. Or being in front of people. I want to be alone with him.

"You want to get out of here?" I ask him.

Gannon looks completely surprised, but his expression turns to one of pure lust within seconds. "Yes."

He's clearly not going to second guess why I'm asking. With the way he hustles us out of the bar, you'd think he was in a race in case I change my mind.

But I'm not. I might not have known what I wanted when I walked into this bar tonight, but the second I saw him, I was absolutely certain.

I'm taking the leap, while holding his hand.

"I don't want to wake Aunt Cher."

Which would definitely happen if Gannon keeps kissing my neck like that. I was going positively insane with lust by the time I fumbled with my keys and got the front door open.

"I can be quiet," he promises solemnly, holding up two fingers like a scout.

"I'm not sure I can," I admit, a ripple of anticipation rolling between my thighs.

"Fuck, Ams, you are killing me." Gannon grinds his erection into my stomach, and I know we need to hurry up.

"Basement." I make the executive decision.

"Who knew that one day I'd be defiling the place where I taught you how to play gin rummy." He chuckles low in my ear, and I smile too.

"That couch has seen more action from other people than it has from you and me." We descend the first step into the basement.

"I'm pretty sure Callum got to second base with Bevan for

the first time on that couch." Gannon's hands squeeze where they hold my hips.

"I think we might make it further than that." I look back at him in the darkness.

"Swear to God, you're going to kill me tonight." His head is thrown back to the ceiling, and I watch as he gulps and his Adam's apple bobs.

When we've finally stepped off the last stair and are alone in the silence of the depths of my house, strong, ropey arms wind around me and pull me flush against a hard chest.

There is still a lot of talking to be done. I need to really tell my best friend how I've felt all these years. He needs to know what I expect from a relationship with him, and I want to voice my worries about what happens if this doesn't work.

But we've done so much thinking, so much arguing, so much passive-aggression the past couple of months that right now? I just want to feel. It might not be the wisest decision, but it feels like the right one at this moment.

"I want to take my time. Spend hours exploring your body. Learn every hidden spot that makes that incredible moan burst from your lips. I'll do that, eventually. But right now, I want to be inside you."

If I wasn't wet before, I certainly am now. My answer is to push up on my toes and kiss him. Once our mouths meet, it's all warm desperation and push and pull. My hands are in his thick brown locks, and his fingers knead at my ass through my jeans. He pulls my shirt over my head, and I do the same to him. Our skin is burning up as it slicks over the other. I need him now, but the couch isn't really going to cut it.

"Hold on."

The nightlight in the corner is the only guide we have as I spread a blanket on the floor with Gannon distracting me. He's peppering my back with kisses, and I'm torn between giving us a landing spot or turning around to take his pants off.

Gannon scoops me up and lays me down, and we make quick work getting each other naked.

I don't need foreplay. We've had weeks of foreplay. We have an eternity to experiment with foreplay. Right now, I want the home run.

My legs spread wide, and I'm practically pulling him into me.

"Condom," he chokes out, because we both know how carried away we can get.

A trail of fire blazes over my skin as he gazes upon me while rolling the protection down himself.

"You're okay from the pill? The morning after ..." he asks, pausing above me.

I squirm, spreading my legs wider so he'll sink down and connect us. "I was okay, Gannon. I promise."

"I hate how stupid I was. I thought so much about our first time, about how special I wanted to make it ..."

Reaching up, I cover his cheeks with my palms. "We can't go back. The way it happened is how it will always be. We might wish we can change it, but I'm glad it happened. Because everything that unraveled got us here. And now, we have a lifetime to make up for that first time."

"Forever. I want forever with you." He groans as he covers his body with mine.

That thick, perfect cock parts me, and I arch my back until my breasts hit his defined pecs. Gannon doesn't stop until he's slid all the way inside me, every inch of him sheathed in my wetness.

"You're fucking perfect."

His hands thread with mine, pinning me to the blanket so that he is in control.

"You are a sight to behold." The words he growls are poetic. "I've dreamed of being inside of you for so many days of my life. Years. I ..."

He seems to get choked up, and even though he's thrusting his cock at a hypnotic pace, this moment is emotional more than passionate. I try to focus, to really hear him, because what he's doing to my body is criminal. I'm dizzy with the sparks of my impending orgasm.

"I love you, Amelie. You are everything in this world to me."

"I love you so much." I breathe, every ounce of truth spilling from my body.

Those eyes, which are hooded with sex, flutter closed, and a small smile paints his lips. "Those are the best words I've ever heard in my life."

Our bodies move in tandem, the need for release and showing each other physical love at its highest peak. We're melding, colliding into one, becoming the us that I've always hoped was in the cards.

And when he steals my breath, I steal his at the same time.

We fall into the obsidian together.

"So, does this mean you'll be my girlfriend?"

Gannon's morning voice is extra sexy and special when I'm waking up next to him for the first time embraced in his arms.

Yes, we've slept in the same bed, but that wasn't romantic. It wasn't intimate or with our limbs entwined when my eyes first fluttered open.

The basement is dark, the only light filtering through coming from the small casement windows.

I'm wrapped in him, both of our backs probably sore from sleeping on the hard carpet over concrete. The blankets we laid down didn't do a lot of good in cocooning us, but I like this better than waking up in my bed. Even though I know Aunt Cher is in her bedroom upstairs, there seems to be separation since we're in the basement.

So, at the same time I feel like a high school kid sneaking her boyfriend in through the basement window, I also love the privacy it affords.

"I'm not sure. We have a lot to talk about still." I say it with full honesty and sincerity.

I can't let myself chicken out when it comes to this conversation. I went into last night hoping that if I built up the courage to go up to him, I would let him know exactly what's been on my mind for years. Just because last night was as close to perfect as we've had, that doesn't mean I can just shove those feelings back again.

A beat passes, and I'm blown away by how he responds.

"You can't keep doing this to me." Gannon lets out a frustrated groan. "You may be confused and upset and going through a lot, but I have feelings too, Ams. I care about you, I care about you so fucking much. And I'm so goddamn attracted to you that I'm practically always walking around the house with a hard-on. I think about you every second of the day. I know I haven't been the best friend or most aware male, but you can't keep leading me on like this. One minute you're all over me, and the next it's like you're allergic to me. Like you can't stand the sight of me. You told me you love me last night. I'm in love with you. What more do I have to do?"

I did not, in the slightest, expect that reaction. He's now sitting fully up, the makeshift blanket bed pooling at his waist.

My head blushes with sympathy. But my heart, the organ of passion and irrationality, beats with anger. This isn't how I was going to start telling him all of the feelings I've had over the years, but I guess it's how we're going to do this.

"*I* can't lead *you* on? Do you even know how hypocritical and ridiculous that is? I've been tagging along after you like a puppy for years. So please, excuse me as I try to sort out the millions of feelings constantly whirling around in my body. Forgive me for going through one of the most difficult times of my life, thinking the only family member I still have is going to die, and not being able to be a hundred percent attentive to the whims of your heart whenever you feel like changing them! You just now realized that you want this, but I've known for years."

Gannon is shaking his head vigorously. "I've known for years. I told you, I never thought I deserved you. I've been in love with you since the beginning, but, Ams, I just couldn't hitch you to my wagon. I couldn't do that to you. You know my family, my upbringing. I had nothing good to offer. So I quietly stepped back, even though I was totally gone over you."

"Somehow, that only makes it worse. Feeling like I've been led on only to know that you secretly loved me, too."

All of those beautiful back muscles ripple as he turns away for a second and takes a deep breath. Things went from cozy and happy to heated in just moments. I nearly have whiplash, because I wasn't expecting him to react like that. And once provoked, my anger came out of left field. Clearly, the bliss from last night isn't going to mask the conversation we haven't had. I know that, but this makes it abundantly clear.

When Gannon turns back to me, he seems more composed. This must have been brewing inside him for some time for him to just snap like that.

"So talk to me. Tell me. I want it all. We've always been able to be honest with each other, you know me better than I know myself. You're it for me, Ams. We have air we need to clear, so let's do it. I'm tired of this elephant in the room standing between us, blocking me from getting you completely. I'm in it for the long haul, so hit me. Where it hurts, if you need to. Get it out so that we can deal with this and move forward. Together."

Knowing he won't go anywhere after I get everything off my chest might just be the confidence boost I need. Gannon lies back down next to me and gathers me in his arms. It almost feels better huddled against his chest, knowing he isn't looking at me as I start.

"It was the first day of eighth grade. Gabrielle Minstro showed up in the same outfit as me, the one I'd spent weeks looking for because I wanted to look so cool. This orange miniskort with a tight T-shirt that had little peaches all over it. I was crushed, because at the time, she had boobs and I had a flat chest. It looked so much better on her."

"One, that's not true. And two, I think you won that battle in the end." One large hand palms my right breast, and his fingers roll my nipple.

A shiver runs down my spine as I press into his touch, but I keep going.

"You found me in the girl's bathroom, just barged right in with no care for who was in there. And you pulled this little piece of fortune cookie paper out of your pocket. It said—"

"Be the star you know you are." He recites it as if the phrase has been tattooed on his memory as well.

My heart catches in my throat because how the hell does he remember this too? "You handed it to me while saying you'd gotten it over the weekend and knew it was meant for me. And that I looked an infinity amount of times better in the outfit. I knew right then that I loved you. Oh, before then I definitely had a crush. But that was the moment it all changed. I was hands down infatuated, enamored. And it only grew. You were my best friend, we shared everything. The more I kept listening to you talk or spent time close to you, the harder my heart fell. I should have sucked it up, should have told you right when I knew. But I didn't want our friendship to change. And then my parents passed, and I couldn't lose you. Hiding my love, keeping that secret, it was better for a time than the risk of losing you if you knew how I really felt. As time went on, however, I couldn't swallow it down as well. I'd start to get jealous of whoever you were dating. You'd make promises and not show up, even if they were the smallest things like grabbing an ice cream cone or sitting with me at a football game. Prom came and went with no dance. Bevan and Taya would tell me I deserved so much better, that if you couldn't see how amazing I was, then you weren't the one for me. But my foolish heart held on."

I take a deep breath, tears pricking my eyes and fuzzy emotions slick in my throat.

"When we got to college, when you decided to enroll at Talcott too, I thought maybe something would happen. But you still treated me like your kid sister, fending off the minimal advances or attention I did get from other guys. You'd build me up to hope you'd finally notice me, and then tear it all down by never taking it to the next level.

"I probably would have kept holding on, pining for you. But then I saw you say you could see yourself marrying Cassandra on the show. That absolutely gutted me. It was the last straw. I felt like someone ripped my heart right out of my chest. I was so angry, I could barely look at you when you showed up for the house meeting at the end of last semester."

Actually, I punched him because I was so angry.

"I decided I was moving on. That I couldn't stand being so heartsick anymore. And just when I was about over you, you backed me into my room and screwed me on my desk."

Gannon's long lashes flutter, and his breathing picks up. "I couldn't help myself."

"Me either. And that scares me. I know you haven't meant to hurt me, deep down I know that. But you have. And I'm genuinely scared, Gannon. I love you, more than I could ever express with words. But what if this doesn't work out between us? I'll not only be heartbroken, but I'll lose my person. I don't think I could live with that. And I have doubts, as much as I don't want to, I think about all of our history. I don't want to be wrong again, not this time. My heart can't handle it."

Gannon's arms secure around me, the hug soothing places in me that words never could. He holds me tight against him for a long time, just soaking in my hurt and transferring it to himself.

"I'm sorry. That's what I owe you, and I know it isn't enough. I wish I could have stepped up and been a man. I wish I showed my feelings to you, committed to you. While the show has brought me one step closer to where I want to be, I hate the toll it took on us. But in another regard, I'm glad it forced us to confront our issues. Everything that's gone wrong up to now between us is on me, believe that. You were never the problem, my love and attraction to you was never the problem. I know it might not be enough, these words, but I can promise you I'll never be so stupid again. Maybe it took realizing that I might lose you to finally get it through my thick skull. I love you, Ams. I'm always going to. I'm not scared of this failing, because I won't let it. Nothing between us is going south, we're not going to break each other. I'm in this for the long haul."

"You can't know that," I tell him.

"But I do. Because you're my person. You're the single most important thing in my life. I'm never letting you, or this relationship, go."

I have to blink back the tears. This is the emotion that I've needed to let out. I know we'll still have a lot of insecurities and doubts to work through, but I have to try. I've been waiting for him my whole life.

"I'm yours. Will you be mine?"

It's by far the most terrifying set of words I've had to speak to date. But I want this, and as Aunt Cher keeps reminding me, life is too short.

"Yes, I'll be your girlfriend."

His answer is to tip my chin up with his fingers and find my lips in the sweetest kiss yet.

Above our heads, I hear footsteps. Then, the creak of the basement door opening has us scrambling for our clothes.

"If you two come upstairs, I might overlook this little sleepover and make you pancakes," Aunt Cher's sarcastic voice echoes down the stairwell.

"Busted." Gannon chuckles.

It's the exact comedic timing we need to break up the heaviness of our discussion. But even with the sensitive topics and years-long history we just unpacked, I feel lighter. It's been a long time coming, getting that off my chest.

Now that it is, I find I'm not angry anymore. I'm not bitter or sour over the winding road we took to get here.

After all, I got what I wanted in the end, right?

Gannon Raferty is my boyfriend. That used to only happen in my dreams.

Thanksgiving comes and goes, then we're back at school for the last month of fall semester before winter break hits.

Talcott has become its regularly scheduled frozen tundra, and students are huddled in their North Faces scurrying to class because the campus refuses to build a real tunnel system in this arctic climate. There is talk that we might get the first snowfall this week, but don't be fooled. Courses at upstate New York colleges are never canceled, even if there is four feet of snow on the ground.

"I should have brought gloves." Amelie is shivering beside me, her nose cute and red as a button.

I pull her against me in the middle of the quad, stopping even though we're kind of blocking traffic.

"Let me warm you up." Bending to brush my mouth against hers, I fully intend to have a make-out session right here.

She lets me get one kiss with tongue in before pulling away, blushing furiously. "You're scandalous."

"No, I just want to show my girlfriend off to the world."

I can't say the word enough, and each time I do, I feel like I'm floating on air. Hearing Amelie's side of things ... it cut me deep. I'd put that hurt in her voice, that pain in her heart. I'm going to spend every day making that up to her now that I'm overcoming my stupidity. How dumb had I been? I could have been loving her, expressing how I feel to her, for such a long time. The only solution is to remedy that.

If that means making out with her in the middle of the quad while people huffed that we are in the way, so be it.

Now that we are officially a couple, I love the freedom of being able to touch her whenever. Snuggling on the living room couch. Holding her as she cleans off her plate from breakfast at the sink. Holding her hand at the Sunrise Diner and pressing up against her on dance floors with drinks in our hands.

Of course, the best part is that each night we're in each other's beds. And I'm able to experiment in all the ways I've dreamed of over the years. With Amelie on top of me, those perfect fucking tits in my face and mouth. From behind, with her cheek pressed to the mattress as my body slaps into her ass. Last night, Amelie crawled over me and turned around to sit on my face while she sucked my cock. I've never sixty-nined much, but with her I think I'll add it to my everyday rituals.

Her body, the sounds she makes, the way she looks into my eyes when I make her come ... I'm addicted. There is no other word for it.

What's better is that I'm in love with her. Sex has always been good. Fun. But the fact that we have such a deep connection brings a whole other level to the intimacy.

My cock is getting hard as we walk, and I'm about to suggest we find an empty classroom to christen when my phone rings.

I pull it out and check the screen, then answer.

"What's up, Quinn?" I pick up my sister's call as I wrap my arm tighter around Amelie's shoulders.

"Tell her I say hi," Ams whispers, hooking her arm around

my waist.

"Ams says hi."

"First, tell your *girlfriend* I say hi," my sister teases. "But more importantly, I have good news."

My heart begins to race, because Quinn doesn't call with news and say it's good unless it's something big. "What is it? Tell me it's from Keith."

I think Quinn purposely makes me wait a few seconds, to torture me. "Yes, it's from Keith."

Rhythmically, I squeeze and release Amelie's shoulder over and over.

"His pilot, the one he mentioned at our lunch? It was green-lit. He sent the script over for you to look at. Says he's not guaranteeing you a role, but wants you to come in and audition for a part."

"Fuck yeah!" I jump up and down, pumping my fist. "Send the script to me. I can't wait to read it. Did he give any audition details?"

"Not yet, says they're setting up the crew now so he'll be reaching out with the casting director's information once they're ready to see people."

Already, my mind is racing. When can I get out to Los Angeles, when can I audition?

"Thanks, Q. You're the best."

"Just remember that when I'm up for salary renegotiation," she jokes and hangs up.

"What was that?" Amelie looks curious.

"I might have a role," I exaggerate, then redirect. "Well, I have a script. For an upcoming project that I think is going to be huge. The director wants me, and I might have a real chance at this."

Amelie's whole face lights up. "Gannon! That's incredible. I feel like this is *Charlie and the Chocolate Factory* all over again!"

My mind stutters for a minute as she hugs me around the neck, and then I grin. "Our seventh-grade play?"

"The one and only. I remember the day you saw your name as Charlie on the cast list when it was announced. Pretty sure you said 'fuck yeah!' then as well." She giggles.

This is why I love this girl. She remembers every moment, has been there with me through all of it. I highly suggest falling in love with your best friend because then you get a sex goddess and someone to laugh with all rolled into one.

"Let me get you to class before you freeze." I take her frigid hand in mine, my mind somewhere in the warm palm trees of Hollywood thinking about the script coming my way.

Later that night, while Amelie is curled in my lap reading a book on the couch in my attic room, I begin to scroll through the script Quinn sent over. Just a few pages in, I can already feel the world coming to life. It's about a couple of high school-aged boys who live at a soccer academy and will be the next stars on the field for their country.

There is one guy in particular, the legacy player with a head full of sins and a penchant for bad decisions, that I connect with. He's far more reckless than I ever was, but I relate to him in that his parents never set a good example or course for him. He has talent, money, and attention, yet he still seeks more. Kingston, the player I'd like to audition for, isn't your typical golden boy. He won't be the star of the series, but he'll be the most interesting. And that's what I want to take on.

With each word, I'm morphing into the scene, becoming the character. I heard Keith at that lunch, and I'm choosing to believe that he sent this to me before a lot of other people.

This is my part to lose. If I get it, I can stop with the influencer posts. I can make some real money for my family. I can break into a business that I've been dreaming of getting in to.

But at the crux of it, if I get this role, I'll be proving to myself

"Come on, hurry up!"

My boyfriend is practically pulling me through the rows of books, looking over his shoulder.

"We can't do this!" I whisper-yell at him but don't drop my hand from his. "I work here!"

Gannon's strides are long and quick, and it takes me practically running to keep up with his pace. "You're off the clock, you just said so."

"That doesn't mean I want my boss catching me doing the nasty." My throat goes slick with anxiety and nausea.

The last thing I need is Mr. Widenmeyer, with his penchant for cloying throat-clearing, discovering me in the throes up against books he asked me to re-shelve when I was on the clock.

"You know the exact places your boss won't check, and won't send any employee to. In essence, it's genius you're the one I'm deciding to pop my library cherry with. You know all of the blind spots." He winks at me.

"Oh, so you were thinking about *popping your cherry* with someone else?" I glower at his back.

In an instant, Gannon stops and hauls me against him. We're

in the middle of the biography shelves, still in a pretty lit up section of the library where anyone could stumble upon us. But it doesn't stop him from pushing me up against the rows of books and kissing the living daylights out of me.

His ridiculously skilled tongue plunges into my mouth, his hands molding to my breasts over my shirt. I'm a goner. I can't help it. The way he kisses is like a tranquilizer dart to the mind, heart, and everything south of my waist; I have no choice but to stand there and take the overwhelming sensations of pleasure cascading over me.

When he pulls back, he's breathing like a rabid animal, and his expression is what I imagine one would look like. "The only woman I ever see is you. I eat, sleep, and breath you. No, I wouldn't take someone else into the stacks. Part of me has always been waiting for you. I'm simply mentioning that it's a bonus you know all of the hidden corners because what I'm about to do to you isn't for public consumption."

Oh. My. I don't think my brain is properly functioning to get words out, and it feels like my cheeks just burst into flames.

Something comes over me, and I realize that we're going to do this. And if we're going to do this, I might as well do it the way I've always fantasized.

Because yes, *obviously* I've fantasized about this.

Grabbing his hand, I pull him along. Of course, I know the spots no one checks, not even my boss because he's too lazy. I wind us up a back staircase and into the periodicals, then turn a corner. The college archives, with old press releases about the university's news and such, are cataloged in a random part of the fourth floor that barely anyone frequents.

Once we're tucked in the back, I haul Gannon against me. Our tongues work furiously, the kisses panicked, sloppy, and oh so hot.

When I begin to sink down, confusion marks his eyes. Until

the lightbulb goes on, and he leans his head back until it bumps a row of books.

"My fucking God …" His hands lace in my hair as I pull his track pants down, that long, glorious cock springing free.

Yes, this is what I've fantasized about. Feeling like a badass, making him come apart under my hands and mouth, in a room full of books. Some people might think that's a weird fetish, but it's mine, and I'm wet just thinking about him in my mouth.

I swallow him in one long pull, his tip hitting the back of my throat as I breathe through the loss of air.

"Fucking Christ, Amelie!" Gannon hisses, his hips thrusting to push him deeper.

Working him up and down, I flick my lashes up so that he's watching me suck him. Our eyes connect, and the power punch of lust in his hooded chocolate eyes sends tingles fluttering to my core.

Gannon reaches a hand under my chin and begins to move my head himself. It's so hot, naughty, and a little wrong that I'm squirming on my knees on the rough library carpet. He's using me to give himself pleasure, and before I know what's happening, I'm being hauled up.

"I want fucking artwork of that. I want to hang it on my wall, you on your knees blinking up at me with my cock in your mouth. Just thinking about it, I could come every time. Jesus Christ, you're so fucking hot."

Gannon is muttering filthy things in my ear as he turns me, pressing my front to the stack of books while reaching around to unbutton my jeans. He pushes them and my thong down just past my hips, and I hear the crinkle of the metallic condom wrapper.

The thought of getting caught only adds to the head rush as he pushes two fingers inside me.

"You're so fucking wet for me that it's sliding down my hand." He bites my neck, actually bites it.

"Please, Gannon ..." I'm practically breathless with the need for release.

My aching clit, the knowledge that we could be caught, and the need to feel him inside me combine for a feeling that has my heart racing. The organ is like a champion horse, and I'm afraid I might pass out before I'm able to come.

Thank goodness he fulfills my request. I brace myself as I feel him, thick and hot, enter me.

"Have you touched yourself thinking about this exact scenario before?" Gannon slides so slowly out of me that I have to bite my own fist not to make a noise.

My other hand is clutching the shelf so hard that my knuckles are white, while his hands are bruising my hips from how tight he's holding us. Then there is the fact that he's trying to be deadly quiet while burying himself deep inside me.

"You wanted me like this, between your books, fucking you like one of the girls in your romance novels." That whisper is hoarse and full of lust.

He's talked dirty to me before, but never like this. Especially in this setting, where anyone could overhear, it has me hurtling toward my climax.

"Please, baby," I beg him.

"Fuck, I love when you call me that." He drops his head to my shoulder and really starts to move.

If anyone is within ten feet of this section, they're bound to hear skin slapping on skin. Gannon is thrusting up into me with such force that a moan or two escape before I can catch them and smash my lips together.

The whole experience has my head spinning, because it's fast and powerful and my knees are trembling as I tumble headlong into my orgasm.

"*Fuck, baby.*" Gannon grunts, stilling himself, and I know he's pumping jets of his release into me.

Once he pulls out, the loss of him leaving me achingly empty, I turn around to see his flushed, smirking face.

"Well, now that we've checked off one of your fantasies, shall we tackle one of mine?"

My God, sex with him is like a sport. One we're getting very good at.

Taylor Swift's *"Willow"* strums through the speakers.

It's a more upbeat melody than I usually dance to, but then again, I'm happy these days. Her pure voice is like honey as I go into a turn, spinning in time to the music and lifting my leg higher as I pull back for a scorpion in the last part of it.

My back is bent, my head is thrown backward, as I raise my arms over my head and connect with the leg I've just swung up. My body inverts to fold while standing, and I turn with my ankle above my head, in my hands.

I'm glad I could get some studio time in today before I have to leave Talcott for a bit. These dance hours are always a therapy session of sorts, and even though I'm in a good mental space, I know I need to process in the way I've always known.

Winter break starts in two days, and all of my finals are done. I'm just waiting for Gannon to take his last one tomorrow before we can drive back to Webton together.

I haven't been back to my hometown since Thanksgiving break. But Aunt Cher insisted I stay at school now that her chemo treatments for this round are done. She'll have a few weeks of rest and then go for tests and scans before her doctors set the new game plan. I'm hoping she feels a little bit better than she has these past months and can have energy for Christmas. It's her favorite holiday, and I want to take her out to get a tree, hot chocolate, and carolers in the park, and all of the traditions we always partake in.

Gannon claims he is going to spend the holiday with us, but I told him that would be rude of him. His mom, who can go crawl into a hole and stay there for all I care, has barely been home. Gannon's been back and forth the past week trying to take care of the kids, especially Fitz. Quinn says their mother has been more absent than usual. It's important that he makes Christmas as special as it can be for them. I'd have them over to our house if it wasn't for Aunt Cher's weak immune system.

He and I both have issues we're dealing with, but we're doing it together. I never realized that once we became a couple, our bond would get even stronger. He's been my best friend for years, yet there is still more I'm discovering now that we're in this new phase.

For instance, that he gets very nervous to run lines, or rehearse. It's so adorable, watching his cheeks pink as he tries to go through a script for the first time. I knew he was talented, but watching him read through the material that Keith Wonderstone sent him ... it's like he is the character he's going out for. Viewers are going to go gaga for him, that much I know. I couldn't be prouder because this is a bona fide role.

Sure, he still has to audition, but I have no doubt he'll be asked to be on the show.

Clapping catches my ear as I hit my final pose, and I whirl around to see my hunk of a boyfriend entering the studio.

"Why are you always watching me dance?" My voice is shy.

"Because I love it. It's a little part of you that you don't share with anyone. And I don't mean to invade your space, but I just love watching you at peace like that. You're so beautiful." He saunters across the room, dropping his backpack and gathering me in his arms.

"I'm sweaty." I squirm as he presses his lips to mine.

"I like you sweaty." Gannon wiggles his eyebrows. "Have you checked yet?"

Shaking my head, I dance out of his arms and over to my bag. Today is the day I'm supposed to find out about my internship. If I get it, I'll be going to New York for the summer to fulfill a lifelong dream, and what I hope will turn into a career after graduation.

"Hold my hand," he says as I grab my phone. "I want to feel your joy when you find out you got it."

I don't open my mouth to say I might not have gotten the internship. That feels like jinxing it, and I want it so badly I can taste it. After a year full of hardship, this feels like something I could control ... and I need that win.

Opening the screen to my email, I try to slow my heartbeat down and prepare myself for disappointment.

"Eek, it's here!" I screech when my inbox refreshes and a message from the internship coordinator pops up. Squeezing Gannon's hand, I open it, and proceed to read.

A beat ticks by. Then another.

"So what does it say?" He bobs up and down beside me.

"I got it!" I press my phone to my chest, unable to breathe momentarily.

There are thousands of students who go out for this internship, hundreds of thousands probably. I thought I'd be a long shot, that my work and effort were there but I didn't have a prominent enough name or background.

"Yes!" Gannon scoops me up, twirling me around like we're the leads in *The Nutcracker* or something. "I'm so fucking proud of you. You're going to slay those Big Apple shelves!"

I giggle at his excitement and let mine run free as well as he spins me around until I'm dizzy. I can't believe I'll get to work in one of the most iconic libraries in the world. I can't believe I'll be living in New York City for the summer. Part of me is intimidated, but I know that Taya and Austin will be there. I know that I'll be exploring a new place, and somewhere I might end up living.

I'm so happy I could burst into tears. The past couple of months have been so hard, and I've been tested on how much I can load onto my back. This feels like karma coming back to me.

But as he sets me down, something occurs to me.

Nothing is official yet, but I think I know what we're both thinking. If he lands this TV show, he'll be going to California. We don't know when, but probably soon. And now that I know I'll be interning at the New York City Public Library, I'll be on the opposite coast.

Gannon seems to be thinking the same thing. "I'll send you Nobu if you ship me Gray's Papaya."

Leaning into him, I inhale his scent. That minty, musky smell is so familiar to me, it might as well be my own perfume. Gannon is what I know, and being thousands of miles away from him will be torture.

"It feels like we just got together." I pout.

I'm not usually one to look at the negatives, but I've been trained in it this past semester. Plus, I'm selfish when it comes to him. We only just fell in love or admitted it to each other.

"Hey, look at me." He wraps his arms around my waist. "We still have an entire semester. We have all of winter break. And you might think you can get rid of me when you move to the big, bad Apple, but I'm not going anywhere. You're going to go to the East Coast to live out your dream, and I'm going out West to pursue mine. That's called growth, that's called maturity. I've loved you from afar for ten years. I think I can do one summer of a long-distance relationship. Plus, we can have phone sex and how hot is that?"

His last sentence makes me smile through the sadness. "You're shameless."

"Only for you, baby." He kisses me on the cheek. "But seriously, stop overthinking this. We'll be fine. We're in love, and we have months. And think of the places we can have sex in the New York library when I come visit. Jot them down when you find them in anticipation of my visit."

"Is it just about sex for you?" I roll my eyes in good humor at him.

"When I watch you dance, yes. And when I touch you. And when you're within twenty feet of me. So basically ... yes."

He swallows my laugh with his lips on mine. This moment feels like a bliss that's a long time coming, and I wouldn't want to share it with anyone but him.

Snow falls outside the window, the fireplace is crackling, and Bing Crosby plays on my phone.

On the TV is a marathon of *Elf*, but Aunt Cher and I are pressed to the glass of the bay window in the living room.

"If you two don't come away from there, your noses will get stuck a la Ralphie Parker." Gannon chuckles at us.

"I just love a first snow. Especially on Christmas, it feels magical." Aunt Cher sighs.

Reaching over, I grab her hand where it rests on the top of the couch. "Me too."

She isn't much better than when she was doing chemo, but her cheeks have a little color. She had enough energy to bake thumbprint cookies today and bring Christmas cards to the neighbors. And we basically just stayed in our pajamas all day eating sweets, baking pies, and watching tons of holiday movies.

It was perfect. And now it's almost over. There is a weird feeling about the night of Christmas Day. All the festivities are over. There isn't anything else to look forward to. The moment still has a little magic, but it's mostly just heading toward business as usual. Honestly? No matter what day it is, the evening hours of Christmas Day are the worst Sunday scaries ever.

We spent the day alone until Gannon came over. I forbid him from spending last night and today with us, even though he tried to convince me. He claimed his siblings wouldn't mind, but we both know that isn't true. Gannon is a good brother, and he provides for them. I know that much. But being in his childhood home is hard for him. The younger kids know a mother who is mostly absent. Gannon has seen her at her worst, lived with her while she dragged him around the country. There have only been a couple of times where he's gotten vulnerable enough to tell me of some of the worst situations they lived through, and I don't blame him for being hesitant to be the caretaker for his family.

In the end, he agreed, but tonight he got the last word. Gannon insisted on staying the night, even though I said he should go home again. But I don't really have a leg to stand on, and plus, I miss sleeping by his side. We're never without each other at our Talcott house, and sleeping alone is strange now.

Christmas always makes me miss my parents, no matter how great Aunt Cher makes it. It's been so long without them that I feel guilty when I can't completely recall their faces. They were wonderful, the best kind of mother and father. Through the therapy I did after they passed, that Aunt Cher made me go to, I've learned to accept the grief, mourn it, and try to make peace with it. Obviously, it's easier said than done. Most days I can wade through it, and be sad but thankful I have a good support system around me.

Nights like tonight, though? I wonder what they'd be doing? Maybe curled up on the couch together, watching Gannon and me? Mom loved to knit, maybe she would have given him a scarf. And Dad would pretend to do his overprotective thing, but secretly love that my boyfriend makes me so happy.

"All right, I'm going up." Aunt Cher rises from the couch, and my attention diverts immediately to her.

I watch her arm shake and instantly begin to get up to help her. But Gannon cuts me off.

"On the arm of a gentleman, of course." He takes her elbow and then winds her arm through his.

"My hero." She blinks up at him, her lashes all but gone.

"I'll get her settled. You relax," he tells me, and I'm pretty sure he's my hero, too.

"Love you, sweet pea." Aunt Cher calls me the name she used to use when I was a little girl.

"Love you so much." A knot of emotion clogs the middle of my throat.

"Now, Cherry, don't get handsy with me," Gannon teases her.

My aunt's throaty laugh can be heard down the stairwell, and I slump back in both worry, wonder, and relief. I've been her primary caretaker when I'm here. While I would never give that up, and like to take care of her, it feels nice to get a break. What's even sweeter is how Gannon is with her. Seeing him assist her, take her up to bed ... it makes me want to burst into soulful tears.

The man I love has the best heart on the planet.

"She's pretty much asleep." He pulls me into him as he settles on the couch.

I watch the snow fall outside the window. "Thanks for bringing her up. She did a lot today, but it didn't look like she was in much pain."

We sit and watch the snow while he rubs my back over my sweater. It's peaceful and content. I used to think that if we ever crossed the line into dating, things would get weird. But they haven't. Actually, much the opposite. We are still best friends, but it's more now. A deeper connection, a stronger sense of what the other person needs.

"I never gave you your present." A large hand massages my shoulders, sending me into a trance.

I frown at him. "We don't do presents."

It's always been a thing. We don't really do gifts. Usually just food, or a trip to somewhere local we've been wanting to go.

"Yeah, well, now you're my girlfriend. So that's changing." Gannon nods like it's final.

"I didn't get you anything." Instantly, I feel guilty.

His lips hover over mine. "I think I know what I'd like, and you can give it to me later."

A delicious shiver runs down my spine.

"But for now, open mine." He hands me a rectangular package wrapped in bright green paper.

"Did Quinn wrap this for you? Looks way too good for you to have done it."

Gannon presses a hand to his chest. "I'll have you know ... that the clerk at the store did it and I paid an extra two dollars for it."

That makes me giggle. But when I open it, my jaw drops with an immediate gasp. "Oh my God, Gannon ..."

Sitting in the box is a book that I've stared at thousands of times. It evokes so many memories, both good and bad, that my heart flashes from hot to cold and back again.

Harry Potter and the Goblet of Fire, the book I'd been in the middle of reading when my parents died. That's what Gannon got me.

"It's a first edition." His voice is quiet as he reaches out to cup my jaw. "I remember you holding on to this for dear life the day after the funeral, like the story could transport you to a different place. That's always stuck with me. I want you to know that whatever tough times we face ahead, we're facing them together. And when I physically can't be with you, hold on to this. It's gotten you through worse, and you've come out on the other side strong and resilient."

"This is ..." I can't even form words, much less breathe.

It's the single most thoughtful gift anyone has ever given me. It's not big or flashy, although I could kill him for spending the money on a first edition. The sentimentality is something only he would know, and the truth behind what it means is something I've shared with him and only him.

"I love you." A tear escapes, rolling down my cheek. "How do I deserve you?"

"I ask myself that about you daily. Have been asking it for years." He shrugs like he doesn't understand it.

That's something I love most: his humbleness. Not being able to see how supportive and wonderful he is makes him the best kind of man because he does it just to give love to others. He doesn't care for those around him to boast about it, or be owed a favor in return.

"You're so worthy." Maybe if I keep repeating it, someday he'll believe me.

Gannon kisses me just as Bing begins to sing "*White Christmas*." Everything in the world is right.

34

The As are filed, and I'm moving on to the last letter names that start with B when I get the phone call.

I hate sorting and re-shelving days. Where the students who work in the library have to go section by section to make sure every book is in the right spot so that our fellow students don't have to go digging. You'd be surprised how much gets put out of place, even with our impeccable system already implemented.

The fiction sign looms overhead as I traverse the aisles, the books in my cart swaying against one another. Spring semester has started and I'm already itching for it to be over. I want to go to New York and start my internship. At the same time, the start of summer means leaving Gannon, if he's going to Los Angeles. My mind is in limbo, and both my job and classes aren't keeping my attention.

I don't notice my phone ringing until I'm actually at the shelf I need to start with. When I pull it from my pocket, Aunt Cher's name is flashing.

"Hey." I smile into the phone as I pick up. "Did you call to keep me company while I do menial work tasks?"

"Not exactly." Her voice borders on upset and is comprised of lingering bad news.

"What is it?" I detect her hesitancy immediately, even though we're miles apart.

I should have known that she'd get her test results this week. But I've been so preoccupied with my own stupid personal life that I clearly forgot. My stomach instantly knots.

"My doctors say that the chemo helped, the tumor shrunk. But ... they think it's shrunk to a size that would be operable now. They want to schedule a surgery to go in and try to remove all of it."

Breathing in through my nose, I try to regulate the air in my lungs. "Okay ... okay. That's kind of good news, right? I know it's surgery, but if they could get all of the tumor ..."

Aunt Cher sighs on the other end. "Yes, it could be considered positive news. I just ... surgery is a big monster. It'll be invasive, and there is no guarantee it'll be successful. I will probably still have to do chemo after, and remission could be months or years down the line."

"But you're going to do it, right? You can't not do it ..." Panic seeps into my tone.

"Yes, I'm going to do it. There are just ... other complications that come with it."

Something dawns on me.

"The surgery, they'll just take the tumor?" I'm waiting for the anvil to drop on my head, but I need to hear her say it.

"They're going to remove my ovaries." Aunt Cher's voice wavers.

I know she's trying to be strong, for me, but this is a devastating blow. I clutch my mouth so that she can't hear the strangled cry I let out into my palm.

"Is there a way to save them?" I ask when I'm able to speak through the unshed tears.

I hear her shaking her head. "No, not if they want to get the whole tumor. And obviously I want that toxic thing out of my body. But everything comes with a price."

"You'll never be able to have children." I state this like she doesn't already know it, but I'm just so dumbfounded and shocked.

"Hey, stop that. I have a child. You have been the biggest blessing ..." Aunt Cher chokes up and cuts herself off.

I drop to my knees in between the stacks, tears dripping onto my jeans as I silently sob. This isn't fair, any of it. She's healthy, she takes care of herself. Aunt Cher is a good fucking person, and I hate the world for cursing her with this. She doesn't deserve any of it.

"But I'm going to fight. We're going to fight. Hopefully, if this is successful, we'll be counting down the days until my hair grows back." Clearing her throat, I can hear her pulling herself together.

I nod my head like she can see me. "I love you."

"I love you, too. Now, tell me how I can distract you from your menial tasks."

She stays on the phone with me for close to an hour, talking about nothing and everything.

This surgery has to work. Because I can't imagine what my world will be like without her.

"I have Keith Wonderstone on the other line."

Quinn's excited hiss travels into my ear from the phone and lights up my entire body. "What're you doing talking to me, then? Put him through!"

My calls are usually forwarded to her, or she gives her contact information so she can filter through the garbage.

"I wanted to give you an air of professionalism, dipshit." I can hear my sister roll her eyes at me. "If this is about the pilot, you go get it. No hemming and hawing."

"As if I'd turn down any chance." I'm getting annoyed with every second she stays on the phone. "Put him through. And Quinn?"

"What?" she snaps.

"Thank you for everything you've done for me." This wouldn't be happening if it wasn't for her.

The phone makes a clicking noise, and suddenly I'm on with Keith. "Keith, it's good to hear from you."

On the other end of the phone, people are bustling and talking, and I think I hear police sirens. "Gannon, I don't have much time. We're running this scene for the thousandth time and I'm pissed off ... Morgan, get your ass to your mark!"

I pull my ear away as he yells.

"Anyway, the script I sent you, we're ready to cast for the pilot. Did you read it?"

The words can't come fast enough. "Yes, and I was immediately drawn to Kingston. I love the complexity of his character and really connect with—"

"We might already have someone we're leaning toward for Kingston. But you can come read, and maybe we'll find another role for you."

Disappointment sinks my heart. I wasn't anticipating that, but Hollywood is a harsh mistress. I don't know what to say to that other than to fight for myself and why I should get the role of Kingston. But I'm a nobody, someone who will take scraps if they're handed to him.

"Come, screen test for us. Worst we can do is reject you." Keith's tone is light and teasing.

He doesn't have to convince me in the slightest. "I'll be there. You say when."

"Two days. We'll fly you out tomorrow. My assistant will send all the details."

Everything in me takes flight. My extremities are tingling, I'm so damn excited that I don't notice Keith has just hung up the phone until I'm profusely thanking him and no one is there. A resolve sits in my gut. I'm still going to make them let me read for Kingston. They'll see that I'm perfect for that role.

I race home from campus, praying I don't get pulled over but also not slowing down. I have to tell Ams, she needs to be the first to hear.

"Amelie!" I shout as I walk into the house, my voice echoing.

"I think she's upstairs. Came storming in and up a couple minutes ago," Scott says from the couch.

He's drinking a beer on a Monday afternoon, and his shirt has mysteriously left. I honestly don't know how the guy manages to stay in academic standing to stay at Talcott. He barely goes to class.

The thing he said about Ams is peculiar, but I ignore it and take the stairs two at a time. "Amelie! You won't believe what just happened ..."

When I fling open her door, there are suitcases on the bed and she's flying around the room.

"Aunt Cher's surgery got scheduled for the day after tomorrow, so we have to pack bags and get up to Webton, and ..."

She's rambling and her petite body is holding as much anxiety as a two-ton elephant.

And my stomach falls through the floor. Cherry's surgery is tomorrow, and she wants me to come with her. To hold her hand in the hospital, to be her support system. On the one hand, I'm elated that I'm the one she wants to be by her side.

But on the other hand ... I just got off of the most career-making phone call of my life.

"Slow down, baby. Slow down." I make her come to a standstill and hold her by the shoulders.

Her gorgeous amber eyes are red-rimmed, and she's practically shaking. She's on the edge of a breakdown, and I need to talk some sense into her, but my own mind is reeling.

"What did Cherry say?" I try to slow my own brain down.

"The tumor shrunk enough that they can go in and get it. So they want to do surgery in two days. But they're going to take her ovaries." She starts to cry, and I haul her against me.

I pepper her forehead with kisses as she quietly sniffles. "I'm so worried, Gannon."

"She'll be okay. This is a good thing. The treatments worked. They're going to get the tumor."

"We have to leave. Today. I want to be with her as much as

possible." Amelie nods as if just thinking about a plan can will it into action.

"About that ..." I start, not knowing how to handle this.

Either way I frame this, she's going to be pissed off. She won't hear me, I get that. But I have to speak up. I'm stuck between a rock and a hard place, and I hate it. But my news matters, too.

"Keith Wonderstone just called. He's finally casting for the script he sent, and they want me to come audition. In ... two days."

She blinks, and not one iota of excitement crosses her face. Inside, I'm wounded. I know what's running through her mind right now, that she's hurting so badly and her anxiety is through the roof. But I was hoping for one second of congratulations. My ego craves it, my need for her to be proud of me so selfish in this moment.

"But tomorrow is her surgery," Amelie says this as if nothing else exists.

"I know that. I swear I know, Ams." I hold her hands. "But this ... this could be it. This could be the break I've been waiting for. If I book this, I could set my family up for life."

"Aunt Cher is having surgery tomorrow," she deadpans, looking as numb as I believe she feels.

"Amelie." My voice denotes all the pain and frustration I feel.

I don't want to leave her. It's the absolute last thing I want to do. But if I don't fly to LA, if I don't screen test ...

"You always do this, pick popularity over me. You did it in high school, you did it when you decided to go on *Mrs. Right.* The allure of fame is stronger to you than my love. I'm sick of coming second to your ego, Gannon. Nothing I do will ever put me first in your book—"

"I'm doing this *for* you. Or for me so that I can be the best kind of man for you! I want to be the kind of man who goes after his dreams, and yes, acting is my dream. A recently realized one, but it doesn't make me any less passionate than you are about your books. I want to be the kind of man who provides for his family. Don't you want me to land this, to support my siblings? Isn't that the kind of man that you want? I want to show you how responsible I can be. Of fucking course I wish I could be here for her surgery. But saying no to this audition would be saying no to my family, and while Cher is my family, I have little kids in Webton wondering who is going to parent them if our mother won't."

She blinks at me with tears in her eyes, and her pert little mouth is turned down in a sad frown. If she cries, it'll be a dagger through my heart, but I know this is the right thing to do. I feel torn in half, warring between two scenarios that are equally important.

"I have to go, Ams. I'm sorry, but I have to do this." I know she can't see why, but I wish she could understand.

"This is more important to you." She shakes her head.

"You are the most important thing to me. I swear to God you are. I love you more than my next breath. But this trip, what I can do there, it could change my life. My family's lives. You can be pissed at me, you can curse my name and blame me, but I hope that when you clear your head, you see that, too."

"Get out. I have to pack." She turns so swiftly away from me that I wobble and almost fall into the wall.

"Amelie ... let me drive you to Webton. I'll stay up all night driving back here to catch my flight, I—"

"I'll have Taya or Bevan drive me. Wouldn't want to ruin your date with Hollywood." Her voice is dripping with acid.

My heart physically aches, as if it's trying to pull itself from my chest and stay with her. But I turn around all the same. I've been there for her through everything.

And try as I might, I can't help but see this as her not supporting me.

"I need more from you. More emotion."

Keith points his finger in my direction, and the back of my neck heats with disappointment.

I've been in this particular audition for half an hour, playing Kingston opposite another male actor who is going out for the lead role of Jude. Jude is the leader of the prep school in the fictional series and will garner the most fan attention. The guy, I think his name is Derek, is pretty good from what I read of Jude in the script.

"Kingston is a bleeding heart, a wounded animal with an exterior full of gloat and ego. You're falling flat, Gannon." Keith looks bored as he says this to me.

I'm bored with me, too. Or, well, pissed off is more like it. Because as much as I'm trying to tap into the emotion I know I need to infuse into these lines, I can't seem to get it.

My head is a mess, and all I keep thinking about is everything I need to get back to on the East Coast. I decided to come here; I decided to go for this instead of be there. It wasn't a selfish choice, it was a practical one, but I can't help the guilt weighing down my soul.

"Let's reset. You get one last shot, kid." He points his finger at me.

Derek looks peeved that he has to play opposite me, and I try to convey an apology. I'd be pissed too, if I had to act with what I'm giving him right now.

For one moment, I turn and let myself breathe. Inhale, exhale, let everything else go. I can dwell on the surgery, on my fight with Amelie, on my siblings back home, on my courses being neglected. There is so much I could let invade my thoughts right now, but I need to focus. My life and career depend on this.

So when I turn back to Keith, who raises an eyebrow and then yells action, my mind is clear. The only thing I see in my head are the lines I need to be speaking, the character direction.

Rolling my shoulders, I transform into the character of Kingston, putting on all of his British cockiness and sinful ego.

"It's *mad* that you're back here, mate," I say to Derek, who is supposed to be playing Kingston's best mate, Jude.

I pretend to dribble a soccer ball, even though I don't currently have one in this room.

"A load of bloody bollocks," He gives me the line back.

"At least you get to see me every day now." I wink, trying to come off cheeky and arrogant.

"That's true, mate." He pats my arm, looking dejected because his character was sent back down to the minors from what would be considered the majors in soccer.

"It's not fair, mate. You're the best player they've got, but Coach Niles just gets pissy when you cock up. As if Luigi isn't out there screwing women outside his marriage, or Dalton isn't sucking coke up his nose like a vacuum. And we all know Jasper is gambling away his entire contract at those underground poker tournaments."

The air I give off is one of pure temper, just like my character is described. Make Kingston mad, and he's like a pit bull about to be put into a ring. Which is why I pretend to launch a soccer ball narrowly past Derek, or Jude's, head.

"Settle down, killer. If you fire balls at our goalie like that today, I'll dye all your underwear pink. Again." Derek smirks a devilish smile. "That was brilliant, actually. I might just do it again for fun."

"Bugger off you." I flip him the bird as the scene ends.

As we say our last lines, Derek is looking at me like he just wiped shit off his shoe and realized he was wearing a red-bottomed Louboutin.

"That was fucking *it*," Keith says, snapping my attention to the gaggle of people at the front of the room who were watching us.

"Much better." Derek nods, and I smile back, appreciative that he stuck with me.

My chest puffs out as I hear Keith's claps, and I know in my heart I just might have won him over. If they had been considering someone else, I'm pretty sure my name is now in the running to make their decision difficult.

I join the other actors and actresses auditioning today where they congregate in the lobby. Most of them know each other from past work, gigs, or just from being out and about in LA. But I'm the outsider, I don't live here, and I barely know anyone.

I was told to stay, even though I'm itching to leave, just in case they want me to read lines with any of the females they're considering for roles. My gaze is constantly fixed on my watch because the sooner I can get out of here, the sooner I can get back to New York.

"You're the *Mrs. Right* kid, aren't you?" A guy who looks to be in his teens points to me.

Gulping, I nod. Reality stars are considered worthless amongst this lot, who grind and struggle to win serious acting jobs. They sleep on mattresses in four-person studio apartments and smoke cigarettes because it's cheaper than buying food. To them, I'm a joke.

Case in point, he doesn't even continue to talk to me but turns to his friend and starts whispering.

After that, I put my headphones in. I sink down against a wall and lean my head back while The White Stripes play in my ears. I don't know how long I'm sitting there until someone snags my attention.

"That's Lukan Holder." The girl next to me smacks my shoulder, and I pull an earbud out.

I look in the direction her finger is pointing, and sure enough, there Hollywood's B-list pretty boy of the moment. He's fresh off an indie film where he basically showed his whole cock, and is getting so much praise for it. The movie was just okay to me, but now he's everywhere. Blowing up on TikTok, a presenter at the Grammy's, and even signed a deal for his own line of underwear with an iconic men's brand.

"What role is he going for?" I whisper to her.

"Kingston, from what I heard."

Fucking great, I mutter in my head. So he's the competition. I could see how the producers and Keith would want him as Kingston. He has a certain bad boy with a conscience air about him, and while he doesn't have golden boy good looks, he has a ruggedness that's almost more enticing. I know what they're looking for, and he could be it.

Let's just hope I wowed them enough to make them reconsider.

Stewing in the lobby only makes me more jumpy, because I wish I could go back in there and plead my case for being cast as Kingston.

Finally, one of the producers comes out and cuts us all loose.

Says we'll be hearing from them in the coming week, and thanks us for our time.

That's it, that's all she wrote. Now, I wait to see if I just landed my dream job.

"You want to come out? We have bottle service at this club in West Hollywood," Derek asks me as I walk out with the herd of auditioners.

Two girls and another guy whose name I forget stand with him. I've met so many people today, I can't keep them straight. A glance at my phone shows that if I could get to the airport and grab a flight home, I could be in Webton before the day is done. I could technically be there for Aunt Cher's surgery and for Amelie.

While it would probably earn me brownie points to go out with other actors, to network and get *in* with some people ... there are more important things. I want this for myself, and to help my family. But I've done what I came to do. And now I need to put on my boyfriend hat and go be with my girl.

"Sorry, man, I have to catch the next flight out. My girlfriend is going through something."

"Ah, he's got a girlfriend back home." Lukan comes out of nowhere, sneering in my direction. "Buddy, if you want to spare her, come to LA with no girlfriend. She'll get eaten alive, or someone else will eat you and she'll find out."

He wiggles his eyebrows, and I instantly hate the guy. He doesn't know me, and if he even knew my girlfriend, he'd know there is absolutely no woman who could compete with her. But I don't say that. I've dealt with guys like him before ... hell, I lived in a house of twenty-five of them when filming *Mrs. Right*.

And right now, he's not my problem. He's not worth it on a good day, but sparing him any kind of tongue lashing would make me even later than I already am. With a nod to the ceiling, I promise the universe that if it lets me win this part over him,

I'll never turn into the self-pretentious asshole so many of his kind are.

My girl is waiting for me, and I need to be back by her side where I belong.

My leg has been jiggling so hard, I fear I might need to get medication if it doesn't stop soon.

The only thing I seem to be able to do is look at the clock on the wall, one that resembles the kind you'd stare at in grade school. I'm doing the same thing I did back then, wondering when it will hit a specific time so I can be free. Not of teachers' lectures this time, but of the feeling that my aunt's life hangs in the balance.

"Can I get you a cup of coffee? Maybe a muffin?" Taya sets her hand on my knee, trying to get me to stop bouncing it up and down.

I shake my head. "I don't think I could keep anything down."

Eating and drinking seem futile, as dramatic as that sounds. But I've been a wreck since they took Aunt Cher back. Though, let's be real, I was a wreck the moment she called to tell me she was going in for surgery.

She's been in the operating room for an hour now, and it will be a long night. The doctor said the surgery could take upward of four to five hours because they want to make sure they have it all and want to run tests when they do get it.

Taya and Bevan, of course, accompanied me home, forgoing their schedules to be by my side. At least someone loves me enough to do that.

"Gannon should be here," I mutter, so angry about it that I can't contain the words.

He left for Los Angeles yesterday, and I know his audition was this morning—not that we've spoken. I'm so angry, though I know it's probably over-exaggerated. I just want my person, and it has me more on edge that he's not here to wait with me. Gannon leaving also brings up a lot of old triggers from our past; him choosing attention over what he could have with me and all.

I watch as Taya and Bevan exchange a glance that makes my gut clench.

"What?" I ask incredulously.

Bevan nods at Taya, probably because Tay will deliver whatever they want to say in a less harsh way than Bev could.

"We wish he was here, too, but ... don't take this the wrong way. He's doing what he has to, Am. He was stuck in an impossible place, and he knew you'd have us. Taking that audition meant way more than just winning a popularity contest."

They know how his mother is, what he's trying to support.

"Unbelievable." I huff, but there isn't any heat behind it. "You guys are taking his side?"

"We're always on your side. But this time, you're just wrong." Bevan shrugs, her bluntness annoying me.

"Jeez, thanks, Bev." I roll my eyes.

"He has been here for you for every step of this. Driving back and forth to Webton when he had a lot to juggle himself. He's never once wavered. Shit, I don't think I've seen him talk to anyone outside our house in months. He sure hasn't partied that much. You know how anti-men I am right now, but the dude has been working his ass off to show you how much he loves and cares for you. It has to be mentioned."

Taya picks up the ball, trying to deliver the message in a more soothing way. "All we're saying is ...we know this sucks. It's scary. But drudging up all of your and Gannon's history and throwing it at him isn't the right thing, not this time. I've watched him love you so well since you guys hashed it all out. Don't lose that, Am. This is just a blip, a sour moment."

The worst part is, I know my best friends are probably right. But I need my anger fueling me right now, even if it's unfounded. Because if it's not anger, it'll be devastation, and I can't afford to fall apart.

"Distract me," I tell them. "I can't sit here thinking about this."

There is silence for a moment, and then Bevan breaks it. "I think Callum is dating someone."

Taya sucks in a breath. "Oh shit. Well, we knew it would happen, right?"

Bevan blinks at us, and then bursts into tears. It's the single strangest thing that's ever happened, because I'm not sure I've ever seen her cry. Get pissed, throw things, scream at her ex, threaten to puncture the tires on his car? Yes, to all of the above. But cry in another person's presence? Never. Not in the decade plus we've been friends.

"I screwed up. I know I did. I lost him because of my own stupid issues, and now he's going to fall in love with someone else. God, even saying it makes me want to bend over and hurl. The thought of him with another girl ... I don't think I can bear it."

My heart breaks for her. The high school sweethearts had a lot of issues, some of which weren't Bevan's. But yes, even though I love her, her issues of abandonment that come from an absent father were constantly projected onto Callum. It was impossible to live up to the standards she set for him, and when he inevitably didn't, they'd fight. Terribly.

Their breakup was necessary, but they both still love each other so much. They're the kind of soul mates who can't stay away from each other, but it's so toxic that they'd burn the world down loving each other.

I get up to sit next to her and wrap my arms around her. She's not much of a hugger, but she leans into me as she sniffles.

"You needed to end it. It had to be done. And I know this hurts like a bitch, but you will get through this. If anyone can overcome the tough times, it's you. You're inspiring about it, actually. Anytime I'm really down, I think to myself 'what would Bevan do?'"

She gives me a small smile as she leans up. "It would just be easier if he didn't go to Talcott. Why did I think that would be a good idea? We should have gone to separate colleges in the first place."

"We'll plan a lot of exit strategies and avoidance tactics." Taya nods in solidarity.

"We really are a mess when it comes to love, huh?" Bevan says.

The three of us huddle close in a group hug while Taya gives us words of wisdom.

"Pretty much. But in the end, we work it out. We believe in love too much to stay bitter over it."

M y eyes are sticky, like they've been glued together, when I try to peel them open.

The stale air of the waiting room we holed up in during the surgery invades my nostrils, and my stomach grumbles. I realize I don't know when my last meal was.

I also realize I'm lying on someone's shoulder and open my mouth to ask Taya or Bevan what time it is.

"About midnight, and I think they're bringing Cher out of surgery soon. The nurse who came in said she'll be in post-op for a while."

The voice that meets my ears is definitely not one of the two I expected. I sit straight up, my head spinning from the sudden movement.

"What're you doing here?" My voice feels like ash in my throat.

Gannon looks exhausted, all of those gorgeous brown locks disheveled like he's been running his hands through them.

"I hopped on the first available flight after the audition ended. I wanted to be here, didn't know if I'd make it. When I arrived, you were asleep, so I told Taya and Bevan to go home. You've been out for about two hours."

I stretch, my neck cracking as I do so, and long to curl back up into him. His warmth transferred to me and left strength in its wake. Just having him here in the waiting room makes me feel light-years better than I did at the start of this day.

I was bitter about him leaving to go to the audition, but now I can't seem to muster any of that anger. I should have just held my tongue that first day he told me about the two events coinciding. I should have slept on it, and then I would have seen that I was being irrational. He made it here in the end, killed himself to not only go after his dreams, but then flew back to help me through one of the hardest days.

Without taking another breath, I grab his face and kiss him. Gannon sighs into me, as if he'd been walking on eggshells even while I was sleeping. His arms slip around me and we both melt into each other.

When I pull back, my soul feels like it's resting.

"I'm sorry. I'm so sorry I couldn't see past my own pain. It was blinding, and I was so scared. I'm still scared. But I'm so proud of you. I want to hear all about the audition. I should have just ... taken a beat. You caught me at the worst moment while I was packing to go home, and I couldn't compute anything else. I'm sorry for being a shitty girlfriend."

"Hey, don't call my girlfriend shitty," he admonishes. "You're not at all. You're a human being, and your response was only natural. I was trying gently to make you understand, but distance probably was the best thing. I ... wish you could have been there with me, too. If I'm upset about anything, it's that I couldn't take *you* with *me*. I wish you could have been in that room. Because I freaking nailed it, baby. But I knew the moment it was over that I needed to get my ass back here. You're my family, Cher is my family. I'd never leave you here if it wasn't necessary."

Nodding, I swipe at my eyes. "I know that now, I'm sorry I slipped back into my old ways for a minute. I want to hear about the audition. What did Keith say? Who else is up for the role? When will you hear back?"

"First, how is Cher?" he asks, wanting the updates they've given me through the night.

With a shaky voice, I tell him of her progress. That the nurse at two hours said things were going well. The one who came out at three and a half said they'd managed to get most of the tumors but that her blood pressure had dropped a bit. They were able to get it back up, though. My breathing becomes less controlled the more I give him the synopsis, and I feel close to hysteria.

"What if she dies? What if she leaves me like they did? I'll be alone." I break into uncontrollable sobs, clinging to Gannon's shirt.

He pulls me in, wrapping his arms around me like vises. Like if I begin to fall, he'll catch me even if it means going down himself.

"Listen to me." He presses a kiss to my hair. "You are not alone. You'll never be alone. Taya and Bevan are your sisters, blood doesn't matter with those two. But even more? You have me. I am your family. I always have been. Since the minute I saw you in the fifth grade, you were mine. I'm keeping you, you have no choice. Come hell or high water, you'll have me. I'm never leaving you, Amelie."

Now I'm kissing him deeper, and thank goodness we're the only ones in this waiting room.

Together, we wait for the news I've been hoping for since I found out my aunt was sick.

After Cherry's surgery, she had to stay in the hospital for monitoring for two days.

When she was discharged, I pulled up to the front, where they wheeled her out with Amelie walking right next to her and then drove them both home. Ams has been mired in her recovery since then, bustling around the house like the busier she is, the quicker Cher will be okay.

I'm trying to step in where I can. I've been back and forth between Amelie's Webton house, Talcott, and checking up on my brothers and sisters. According to Quinn, Mom showed up last week for the first time in a month but I missed her. I need to have a chat with her, really sit her down and talk about what's going to happen moving forward.

If I'm in LA and Quinn graduates and wants to move out there, something will need to change. I'm not going to pull the kids out of their schools or the house that some of them have known as their one and only home. But I'm also not going to hold myself back because she can't be a proper parent.

It's not so much that I hate my mom. It's that I both pity and am cyclically frustrated with her. She's not evil, and she isn't malicious or intentionally a bad parent. It's just that she became a mother way too young, and I'm not sure she ever wanted to be one. My mother doesn't have the maternal instinct, she's not even a very nurturing person when I come to think of it.

So I can't blame her for the curveballs life has thrown her. Do I loathe that she couldn't suck it up for her kids and try to be better? Yes. But can I give her credit for trying even when she always seems to fail? Yes, in that regard, too. She just needs to be set straight again, at least until her kids are old enough to take care of themselves without an adult living under the roof. I think my newfound financial success, if I land the TV show, should entice her with enough bribes to keep her around.

There are so many things I'm dealing with that some days it makes my head spin. I'm kind of thankful for them, though, because it takes my mind off of the phone call that hasn't come yet.

It's been about a week since my audition with Keith and the producers, and I haven't heard a word. I'm so antsy about it that I can barely sleep. The only way I'm able to is when I lose myself in Amelie for hours and then fitfully drift off with her in my arms. It means so much, landing this part, and I feel like I'm hanging over a precipice.

"Hi." Ams walks into the living room of her childhood home, where we're staying for the night.

But instead of sitting next to me and snuggling into my nook, she straddles my lap. Instantly, I'm alert everywhere. We're like bunnies, fucking every day of the week and twice if we miss a day. I guess when you wait ten years to sleep with someone, that's bound to happen.

"Hi, baby," I whisper into her mouth before taking it.

My tongue licks over hers, sliding into her mouth. She tastes of the strawberry lemonade she must have been drinking, and the tart sweetness spurs me to take the kiss deeper.

"She asleep?" I ask quietly.

Amelie nods before going back in for more. If Cher is asleep, it means she can't get out of bed upstairs. Her stitches are still in and she needs help to do most things.

But what that means for me is that I can take Amelie's leggings off and spread her wide open without anyone walking in.

Cradling her back, I shift so that I can lay her down and press my hard-as-steel cock into her pelvis. She squirms against me as her mouth finds my collarbone and nips at it. She knows that when she skates her teeth across that spot, I go a little wild.

Like now, when that move spurs me to action. I undress her quickly, wanting her taste in my mouth so badly that I'm almost seeing stars. This is how it is between us, everything escalates quickly. I always mean to go slow, set a pace, but she drives me batshit.

"Need to taste you, baby," I growl, moving down her body.

All of Amelie's gorgeous curves wink at me as I go, and I nearly come when I look up from between her thighs and see her rolling her nipples between her fingers. I'm a dead man walking anytime I eat her like this, because I'm a goner before my mouth even meets her slit.

She's dripping wet as I ease a finger in, and I know she's trying to be quiet with her aunt upstairs.

"Oh God ..." she squeals with the first suck of her clit.

My lips, tongue, teeth, and fingers move in tandem, working her rapidly. The moment her legs begin to quake and she wants to pull me up by the shoulders, I double down. She wants me inside of her, but I want her to come on my tongue.

"Baby, I want to taste it. Give me it," I demand, my voice hoarse.

"Gannon!" she hisses as her hips buck.

And then she's climaxing, her thighs spreading impossibly

wider as I fuck her with my fingers. I'm on my elbows, watching her face. Amelie orgasming is the single most erotic thing I've ever experienced.

Only now do I spring up, positioning myself between her thighs. Amelie licks her lips and my balls seize up.

"Shit, I have to get a condom."

My backpack is in her room, and I sigh knowing I'll have to walk up the stairs with my raging hard-on. But before I can rise, Amelie grabs my elbow, holding me in place.

"I'm clean. I'm on the pill. I trust you."

I hover above her, every muscle in my body trying to urge me forward to be inside her. Those three simple sentences show how much faith she has in me, how much love exists between us.

"You know I would have done right by you if we hadn't gotten the morning after pill, right?" I don't know why I say this.

It's the least romantic thing I could admit at a time like this, but for some reason, it's been on my mind.

"And not because I would have had to. But because I'm in love with you. I always have been. I think about making babies with you some day. Not anytime soon, but you're the only woman I'd ever want children with. If that happened that night, so be it. I would have welcomed it. Because even if we didn't know it back then, they'd have been made of love. I plan on spending my entire life devoted to you. I want to marry you someday. I want our family."

I'm blurting out things, lost in the moment, but every word is true. I need her to know how much I love her, how I'm always going to take care of her.

"I want all of that, too. I'm yours, Gannon. Always have been."

At her go ahead, I slide into her bare. She's the only one I've ever done this with, the only woman I'll ever be with again.

Being connected in this way is like coming home.

"Do you think football players pee during the games?" Taya squints at the TV, her beer dangling from her fingertips.

"No, babe. They just go in their pants." Austin has her in his lap.

He's up for the weekend, and we're hanging out watching Sunday football in our Prospect Street living room.

"Gross!" Amelie looks disgusted. "Does that mean the whole field is just like one big dog park? Just pee and poop everywhere?"

I crack up, taking a sip of my own beer. "I mean, I guess they could hold it until half time. They are adults."

"But sometimes you really have to go. Like you know when you're driving in the car, and the urge just comes on, and you know you might have to pull over ..." Bevan explains, waving her White Claw around.

"Oh my God!" Taya starts to crack up. "*Yes*."

"One time, I pulled over and had to get a towel out of my trunk." Scott nods his head.

"You guys are way too comfortable with each other." Austin shakes his head, chuckling.

"Welcome back to the loony bin, dude. Last week, I got trapped in a conversation about whether regular tampons sold better than super tampons, and how big the average vagina was." I hang my head, scarred from that discussion for life.

"It's a decent question," Amelie points out.

They start discussing if football players take Imodium before games, but I'm distracted by my phone ringing. When I look at the screen, the area code flashing is a Los Angeles one.

I squeeze Amelie's thigh and begin to rise, sending her a look. In an instant, I know that she knows this is the phone call about the role.

"This is Gannon," I answer in the silence of the kitchen.

"Gannon, this is Jenny Illins, one of the assistant producers for *Rogue*. I wanted to call to give you some news about casting."

I swear, I'm floating above my body. This moment feels surreal, and I can either fly high as she tells me that news or come crashing back down to earth.

"Yes, thanks for giving me a call."

"We had many people audition for each role, and I know you were going for Kingston. I just sent an email to your agent—"

Who she has no idea is my barely legal sister, and the thought makes me crack a smile. It always does whenever someone in the industry talks about my agent.

"Congratulations, Gannon. You're our Kingston."

Her words ring in my ears, and I shake my head as if clearing cobwebs.

"I got it? You mean, I'm going to be playing him?" I'm dumbfounded, which is why I ask the glaringly stupid question.

I hear her chuckle. "Yes, you'll be playing Kingston. Like I said, I sent an email over to your agent with more details. We'll need to get you in contract talks with the lawyers and go through all the usual proceedings. But filming starts this summer. Congratulations, Kingston. Welcome to the show. And buckle up."

She has to know this is my first serious scripted show and role. I'm flabbergasted, and all I can do is thank her before she hangs up.

Well, Quinn is really going to have to learn on her feet this time. Contracts for a multimillion-dollar show and all that comes with it? Things are about to get complicated, and I welcome it with open arms.

I stand there, staring at my phone, for what seems like an hour. Every emotion possible runs through me. Elation that I've gotten what I've worked for. Fear that I won't be able to play Kingston well enough. Excitement that I'll be moving and shaking in Los Angeles. Absolute sadness that it will mean time away, a lot of time probably, from Amelie.

"So?" Amelie edges into the kitchen as I stare at the phone in my hand.

I don't bother saying anything. I just walk over to her and throw my arms around her until I'm lifting her off the ground and kissing her senseless.

"I guess that means you got it?" She claps as I hold her up on my waist.

"You're looking at Kingston." I puff my chest out, brushing it against hers.

"Baby!" she cries proudly, then dives in for another kiss. "I'm so happy for you. I knew you'd get it. I'm not sure there is a person alive whose ever said no to you."

Her joy brings me joy, and I can't believe I get to celebrate this with her as my best friend and the girl I love. But that only serves to fuel my anxiety and sadness over leaving her.

"But I'm going to California." My tone is weary.

I've been the one comforting her when we talked about this

before, when she found out she got the internship in New York City. And now, apparently, it's my turn to be hesitant. We have a month or two left at school, and then we'll be separated for who knows how long. I have no doubt in my mind about staying together, but I'm going to miss her so fucking much. She's my other half, and I can't go long without her.

"And we promised we'd mail food back and forth. We'll be okay, Gannon." She rubs my cheek, still straddling my waist like I could carry her around all day. "It's going to stink, but I love you. We'll make it work. We'll take red eyes and I'm always a call away. You can even write me love letters, I *love* that idea."

Note to self, write love letters.

"Plus, there is always FaceTime sex." She wiggles her brows at me.

"Yes, we can get very good at that." I rub my nose against hers with a wolfish grin on my face.

I'm not sure what will happen with school or whether I'll finish. I've always promised myself I'll get my college degree, because I feel my mother's life has been so hindered not having one. It's something tangible to fall back on, and if I've learned anything from my absent parent, it's that I'll never quit anything.

And I'm not sure what will happen with the show. For all I know, it could flop. I could have fought hard for Kingston, and critics or viewers may not even like it.

Or it might take off. This kind of money will be life-changing, but I've also tasted what fame is like. A small amount, where I can still have a normal life and be relatively free in my activities. If the show is successful, which with Keith at the helm it should be, my life will change. I'll be famous, but in a way where people want to track my every move and dig into my private life. I'm ready for that, but I'm scared for the people I love. They didn't sign up for it, and Hollywood can be a cruel beast.

As long as we stay us, the same Amelie and Gannon who

found each other in fifth grade, we'll be fine. She grounds me, she's the one person I can turn to, to not only love me unconditionally but to tell me the truth even when I don't want to see it.

I've been through tough shit before. I've been poor, and I've been the underdog. I've pined for a girl I didn't think I deserved, and I've taken care of the people in my life.

This is the good part, where I start achieving things I want. I need to remember that.

With Amelie having my back, I always will.

"Did you throw the stuff in the freezer away?" I shout to Taya through the open door as I drag the recycling can to the curb.

"I can't believe we're cleaning this place out again. This year has gone by in a second. And yes, I trashed it all." She joins me on the porch as I walk back up.

"Senior year, and we'll be back in this place." I glance at our front door, already missing the Prospect Street house.

It's crazy to believe we only have one more year of college. It feels like just yesterday that we arrived at Talcott, naive freshman who thought we'd already figured out the world.

We're packing up the house and getting it ready for its idle state while we all go away for the summer. Taya and I are headed for internships in New York City, while Bevan is going to Chicago for hers. Scott is going back to Webton to coach youth tennis at the country club, and Gannon is headed to California to shoot his first TV show.

He's so nervous and excited at the same time, it's epically cute. The buzz has already started, and his inbox has been flooded since the announcement was made that he'd be starring as Kingston. I just know he and the show are going to blow up. It's strange that it's all happening because I never had a doubt it would. But it's just weird that it's here. I knew since the moment I met him, Gannon was destined for the limelight.

To me, he'll always be my first love, the boy who knows every part of me. I can't wait to see where he takes this. And I also can't wait for the summer to be over and be back at Talcott with him.

He's going to try, as hard as possible, to attend college next year and graduate with the rest of us. I'm sure that plan will be severely tested at times, with flights and events and red carpets, but I know how important this is to him.

"That's all she wrote, folks." Gannon walks out to the porch rolling two oversized duffels on wheels.

Immediately, my eyes get misty. "Did you grab your passport, just in case? And I threw together a little bag of snacks in case you need—"

He kisses me full on the mouth to get me to stop rambling. I sigh into his lips, calming a little but still wound tight.

"Thank you for making it, babe. I got everything. Don't worry, I'm a grown-ass man, I can handle it."

"Says the guy who forgot to bring his license last time we went to the bar." Taya chuckles under her breath.

He narrows his eyes at her. "Hey! I was distracted. Amelie decided to wear that black dress, and it scrambled my brain."

I blush a deep red and burrow myself into his chest. Squeezing his solid mass of a torso, I soak in our last minutes together before his cab shows up to take him to the airport.

"I'm going to miss you so fucking much." He kisses my neck, and I hear the front door close behind us.

Taya must have given us a minute, and I secretly hope she's cleaning the toilets so I don't have to. Bevan is in charge of cleaning the stove and laundry machines, while Scott is setting up the mouse traps and bug tape for when we leave. We like to keep our house clean, but the place is essentially a college dump that is like a hundred years old and has all kinds of holes for critters to make their way inside.

"I don't want you to leave." I pout, though I don't mean it.

Of course, I'm going to miss him, but I want him to go live out his dreams. My boyfriend is going to be a superstar, not that I ever had any doubt.

"Got you this." He pulls something out of his pocket, and I open my hand.

In it, he places a simple woven bracelet made of white and red string. And it looks so familiar.

"Oh my God, is this the friendship bracelet I made you at summer camp that one year?" I'm so shocked he kept it. I can barely believe I'm holding it.

Gannon nods. "It broke off my wrist about a month after you put it on, and I was devastated. Didn't have the heart to throw it out, and it's been in my room at home all these years. I figured you should wear it now, since it'll fit if I tie it. But let's call it a love bracelet."

He fastens it around my wrist as I hold it out. "I must have known even then, you know with the red and white string and all."

"You had a crush on me." He winks.

"I had more than a crush." I bat my eyelashes.

"Good. Because that's the summer you got boobs, and the image of you in that red floral bikini top was cause for many a boner." That grin is devilish.

"Oh my God." I throw my head back and laugh.

The cab pulls up, honking its horn, and my heart lurches.

"I'll see you in a couple of days?" He rocks us back and forth, brushing my hair behind my ear.

He has to fly to California for part of the week to get some of his costumes fitted for the series. They're starting shooting in another month, and all of his fictional soccer uniforms will be tailored to him.

But the reason he'll be back just days after he flies out there is because we're having a party. For Aunt Cher.

She's officially in remission.

I bawled my eyes out when she rang that cancer-free bell in her doctor's office three days ago.

Her surgery was a success, they were able to get the entire tumor, and then came another round of chemo that lasted eight weeks. It was almost worse than the first, and there were times she told me she was too weak to even open her eyes.

But she made it, she did it. She believed, and I helped her believe, even in the darkest of times. Her cancer will leave her with lasting scars, reminders, and losses, but Aunt Cher never stops seeing the good in life. I think that's where I get it from, and I thank God she was the one who became my guardian. My life could have taken a very different turn after my parent's deaths.

I nod, a lump forming in my throat. "I'm so proud of you. I'll miss you every second."

"I love you so much." He kisses me, a searing, lingering gesture.

"I love you more."

Gannon frowns comically at me and shakes his head. Our hands try to hold on, our fingertips dragging as he walks down the porch steps. I stand there, watching him load his bags and wave at me from the window. I don't head back inside until the car disappears off the street.

Taya is right; this year has gone by in the blink of a second. But it's also dragged on, prolonging the difficult times.

In the end, though, I would never change a single thing. Even Aunt Cher getting sick. Each and every moment, decision, and action led me to the place I'm in right now.

I admitted my true feelings this year, and that love was returned by my soul mate. My aunt overcame the odds and we came out of it with an even stronger bond than we had going in. Her illness gave me a new lease on life, and taught me to not only not take things for granted, but go for every single thing I want with vigor.

In three weeks, I'll be starting my internship in a city that makes dreams come true. My boyfriend is about to go star in a television show. We'll kick long distance's ass and be reunited soon enough. And some day, like he said, he wants to marry me and have a family.

Who knows what the future holds from day to day, but I do know one thing.

I've built a life that I truly like living, surrounded by people who care and support me through everything.

At the center of that is a love for the ages, fought for and struggled over, that will be unbreakable no matter the challenges thrown our way.

EPILOGUE
AMELIE

One Year Later

"Everyone is staring at us."

Bevan grits her teeth in my direction, Taya on one side of her and her boyfriend on the other.

"It's because of superstar here." I hike my finger at Gannon, who sits beside me holding my other hand, and shrug. "I didn't think he'd even be here, so I'll tolerate the gawking. But get used to it. It gets so weird if you pay too much attention to it."

I never thought I'd become accustomed to so much interest or attention being thrown at me, but I guess you compromise when you're in love. The first season of *Rogue*, the TV show Gannon plays Kingston on, had its finale a few months ago, and the world is gaga for it. His face, and all the other people in the cast, are plastered all over the Internet. Gannon is on talk shows and morning hours and in social media campaigns for the network. He promotes *Rogue* merchandise with his character's likeness, gets invited to swanky parties, and was even asked to join a celebrity soccer tournament for charity because of his time spent on the show.

But still, as always, when it's just us ... we're *us*. Sitting here at our college graduation, holding his hand, I feel the exact same way I did when we were in high school going to get frozen yogurt after the final bell.

"I'll soak it up." Scott waves, like he's the King of England or something, at the people gawking at my boyfriend.

"You would." Taya laughs.

She's searching the stands for Austin, who is sitting with her family. Aunt Cher is up there with them as well, along with Gannon's siblings and Bevan's mom. After we walk across the stage, we're all going to the Sunrise. Gannon rented it out just for our friends, for our last time at the diner at Talcott. I didn't even freak out about whatever he paid to do that because I'm so sentimental about leaving this place.

"I'm a civilian today," Gannon jokes, leaning over to me and whispering low so no one can hear. "Think we should make out and give them a show?"

The blush that steals over my face is hot and prickling. "Gannon ..."

We've had countless paparazzi photos of us taken. It's inevitable, but it never gets easier for me. I'm an off-the-grid kind of person, and having people wanting to know every detail of our relationship is strange to me. Gannon usually tackles the brunt of it, and does so respectfully, but I like to reserve our affection when it's just us. But today? I'm just so happy he was able to attend and graduate on time.

So when he kisses me full on the mouth, I give it right back. Our tongues meet, and eventually one of our friends wolf-whistles and I back off.

"Damn, that was hot." Taya sighs. "Wish Austin was sitting down here."

"As if you're not moving in with him next week." I chuckle.

She nods excitedly. "That's true. And we'll see you in a month!"

Austin and Taya are moving into a bigger apartment on the lower east side of Manhattan, while Gannon and I are renting a place in Tribeca. I'm so excited, I can't stop smiling when I think about it. We went to look at it last month before signing the agreement. It's almost an industrial-type building, one whole wall of our apartment is brick. With big windows and lots of natural light, the place feels very old world. I can't wait to make it our own. *Our* apartment, just the two of us. It feels surreal, and very grown-up, to think about it.

It's not like we haven't lived together in our college house for three years. Or like I haven't gone to stay with him in the house in Los Angeles he rents. That place is a palace compared to anywhere I've ever lived.

That's where we'll be for the next month, since Gannon has some promotional events he has to do for *Rogue*. Watching the show, seeing him act in it ... it's incredible. I get it now, why he wanted to pursue this. He's damn good, and the show is absolutely addicting. Watching his on-screen love interest and him is still weird, but I know it's for the cameras. There is something magnetic about Gannon that pulls you in from the second his British accent hits your ears ...

And yes, I've made him do that accent in the bedroom.

I'm going with him for the month in Los Angeles since my job at the New York Public Library doesn't start until July. They brought me on after my internship, and I'll be an assistant librarian in the fiction section. The place is so big that there are several dedicated librarians to each part. I'm itching to start, to be surrounded by my favorite things, books, all day long.

Quinn is currently occupying the LA house and will stay there with us throughout the month. The rest of Gannon's brothers and sisters are still in the house, albeit with a stable au pair he found.

The situation is better than the one he grew up in, but it's still unstable. His mom rarely shows up, and he is straddling a precarious line. He doesn't want to move them out of their environment, but fighting for guardianship would mean he'd have to move them ... when he himself is always on the move. For right now, we're hoping they can all make it to high school graduation without the state catching on, so that their lives will be as normal as possible.

Of course, Gannon will be back and forth most months. He says he'd like to try out for something on Broadway in a few years, to stay put in the city, but who knows. I have a feeling this show is going to take him to heights neither of us can imagine. I'm trying not to look too far ahead.

If going through everything with Aunt Cher taught me anything, it's that we have to be grateful for what we have at that exact moment. Right now, I have an amazing job in the greatest city on earth, where I'll be living with the boyfriend who I'm madly in love with.

Looking up into the stands, I spot my aunt and wave. She whistles with her fingers in her mouth, her excitement palpable.

I won't be far from her for long. After kicking cancer's ass, Cher decided to box up and sell the house in Webton. She's moving to New York City to start her new single life. Her days of looking after me are over, not that she'll admit it. But I don't need a guardian, and she's healthy with a world full of options. Her one-year check showed she's still in remission, and she no longer has to stay in Webton for my benefit.

The fact that she's moving to NYC and we'll be able to grab lunch downtown only makes my move that much sweeter.

"Here we go." I reach over to squeeze Bevan, and then Taya's, hand.

"I can't believe we won't live on Prospect Street anymore." Bevan's lower lip gets wobbly.

"Is she crying? I never thought I'd see the day." Gannon

looks baffled.

"It's a new Bevan, man." Her boyfriend smirks.

My heart swells as I look over our row, all of my friends banded together one last time. After today, we're going to split off and go our separate ways. Sure, we'll make time to see each other, but it won't be the same. I'm both elated for the next chapter and tremendously sad that our college days are over.

Walking across that stage, hearing Aunt Cher yell at the top of her lungs, it makes me teary. I pause in the middle, my degree in my hand, and look up at the sky. I hope my parents are watching today. I hope they know how happy I am, even after the loss I've experienced. I hope they know I'm so loved, that Gannon has exceeded even my wildest dreams about what he'd be like as a boyfriend.

When I get back to my seat, I take his hand and lace our fingers together. My head tilts until it's resting on his shoulder, and I feel him kiss my forehead.

It's a while before the rest of the ceremony is over, but in my mind, I'm replaying all of the best moments we've had at Talcott.

Finally, we're walking off the football field in search of our families.

"Pancakes at Sunrise?" Taya says, getting on with the scheduled program.

One last meal with my friends at our college diner sounds like the perfect tribute to this place. Around the circle, everyone nods their head in agreement.

"We'll meet you guys there in a little, okay?" Gannon takes my hand.

"Where are we going?" I ask curiously.

"Yeah, what the heck? Ditching us because we aren't cool enough? Didn't you book this thing?" Scott flips him off.

Gannon rolls his eyes. "Shut up. I just want a minute with my girl. We'll be there soon."

I bid my friends goodbye for now and follow the boy I've been in love with pretty much since the day I saw him.

"All right, Mr. Mysterious. What's up?"

Gannon pulls me to him, wrapping an arm around my shoulder as I nestle into his hip and breathe him in. This is one of my favorite spots in the world.

"I want to take you to the airport. Our spot, alone, away from the world. It's about to get even more crazy once we leave this place, and I want you to know ..."

He breaks off, clearing his throat. I think back to a time when we couldn't be honest with each other. When we were hiding our feelings and pretending not to love each other to the depths of our souls.

Now I know what he's thinking at all times. There is nothing we don't share. Today feels monumental, an epic moment neither of us were sure we'd reach. My life was a mess just a year and a half ago, and I seriously considered leaving school when Aunt Cher got sick. Gannon has had to work doubly as hard to achieve the dream of getting a degree. Online classes, flying back and forth, and staying up late nights to get the work done. But he did it. We did it.

"You are the single most special person to me on the planet. I don't know where I'd be if you hadn't been right there in front of me in that fifth grade classroom. Definitely, not here, that's for sure. I don't know where I'd be if you hadn't forgiven all my bonehead moves, if you hadn't agreed to love me as fiercely as I love you. Our life isn't going to be conventional, but then again, you never have been. You're a wonder, Ams. Thank you for sticking with me through all of it."

He leans down and captures my mouth, my heart fluttering

like it's our first kiss. Every time, it's like the organ in my chest can't believe he's kissing me.

To me, it's always been us. We'll always be those two kids on the playground, sneaking off to bake mudpies by ourselves.

No matter what happens in this life, he's always going to be my person. The rest of the world can have Gannon the star, but I'm the only one who knows the real him.

I'm eternally lucky that I'm the one he chose to show that to.

———

T hank you for reading! If you loved this book, read Taya and Austin's story in Then You Saw Me!

ALSO BY CARRIE AARONS

Do you want your **FREE** Carrie Aarons eBook?

All you have to do is **sign up for my newsletter**, and you'll immediately
receive your free book!

Then, check out all of my books, available in Kindle Unlimited!

Standalones:

If Only in My Dreams

Foes & Cons

Love at First Fight

Nerdy Little Secret

That's the Way I Loved You

Fool Me Twice

Hometown Heartless

The Tenth Girl

You're the One I Don't Want

Privileged

Elite

Red Card

Down We'll Come, Baby

As Long As You Hate Me

All the Frogs in Manhattan

Save the Date

Melt

ABOUT THE AUTHOR

Author of romance novels such as Fool Me Twice and Love at First Fight, Carrie Aarons writes books that are just as swoonworthy as they are sarcastic. A former journalist, she prefers the love stories of her imagination, and the athleisure dress code, much better.

When she isn't writing, Carrie is busy binging reality TV, having a love/hate relationship with cardio, and trying not to burn dinner. She lives in the suburbs of New Jersey with her husband, two children and ninety-pound rescue pup.

Please join her readers group, Carrie's Charmers, to get the latest on new books, exclusive excerpts and fun giveaways.

You can also find Carrie at these places:
Website
Amazon
Facebook
Instagram
TikTok
Goodreads

Printed in Great Britain
by Amazon

75641844R00166